I0717828

NOAH FINN &
THE ART OF CONCEPTION

A NOVELLA

E. RACHAEL HARDCASTLE

Also by E. Rachael Hardcastle

Fiction

Finding Pandora: The Complete Collection
Aeon Infinitum: Run For Your Life
Bluetooth & the World Wide Web
Noah Finn & the Art of Suicide
Noah Finn & the Art of Conception
Forgotten Faith

Non-Fiction
The Universe Doesn't Give A Sh*t About Your
Book: A Brutally Honest Guide to Self-Publishing

© 2020 E. Rachael Hardcastle

All rights reserved. This book or any portion thereof may not be reproduced or used in any manner whatsoever without the express written permission of the publisher except for the use of brief quotations in a book review.

First Edition

ISBN: 978-1-9999688-6-1

Also available as an e-book.

Curious Cat Books
West Yorkshire, UK

www.curiouscatbooks.co.uk
www.erachaelhardcastle.com

"Sometimes even to live is an act of courage."

Lucius Annaeus Seneca

PART ONE

The Accident

Chapter One
MARSHAL'S DEATH

December 24th 2023

It's 11:59 pm.
And there are two things Maria Shephard knows for sure at this moment.
One: there is no God.
Two: she will die on Christmas Day.

Noah Finn, the entity standing alongside her crumpled car and shaking his head, understands. Maria is angry with him. He's angry at himself, but there's nothing he can do.
She forces her eyes open and blinks—she *has* to stay conscious; she *has* to confirm if it worked. *Then* she can let go.
Then I can let go.

In the background, Maria makes out a muffled, crackling version of 'We Three Kings' on her radio, played beautifully by the violin. Delicate hands lean in and cup her face, then pull away covered in red.

"Stay with me, Maria," a man says. "We'll fix this. I'm here."

There are flashing lights in her peripheral vision. Speech is torturous but necessary as the voice behind them asks if she can move her legs.

She hates that she can't.

She hates that she's still here.

Marshal Shephard, the man in the passenger seat, isn't moving or speaking. But he's looking directly at her. He would want her to be honest about what happened here. She's in tremendous pain but tries to mouth she has no movement at all from the waist down, lifting her fractured wrist to gesture at Marshal in an attempt to check if he's breathing.

Her lips, quivering, part to ask the man Maria assumes is an EMT. He glances past her through the window at his colleague wearing an NYFD uniform, attempting to remove the roof of her car.

Neither of them says anything.

Maria's chest tightens, crushed beneath the

weight of an awful secret.

She heaves an excruciating breath, then sobs uncontrollably.

Noah checks his watch.
It's almost time.

He's been with Maria since her birth and Marshal since his a few years later. He feels nothing for either of the siblings—not deeply, anyway. Sometimes he wishes he could, but he can't. And it's a blessing; this would break any human heart. If he expressed anger, guilt or love towards anyone but himself—because technically he's to blame here—he'd be just as pathetically mortal as they.

And, goddamn it, he isn't.

Noah cannot easily define who or what he is. Most of the time he doesn't try. But, as he crouches and reaches to touch Maria's shoulder to start their meeting, he can sense her panic through the quickening pulses in her aura. No doubt she imagined this would be the easiest day of her life—the end of her suffering. Now, it's memorable for the wrong reasons.

Maria's tragedy *is* a tragedy, though. Not an exaggerated moment of poor luck.

A tragedy.

Her eighteen-year-old brother, Marshal, takes

his last breath.

The accident has completely destroyed the car. Her body is ruined, as is her future. And now her little brother is dead. There is no other word to describe Maria's situation *but* 'tragic'. It's perfectly fitting.

And this single word so accurately defines the thousands of thoughts and emotions all passing through her in less than a millisecond.

How can any human recover from this?

Noah pauses beside her as they attempt to remove Marshal's body, allowing Maria a few extra seconds to witness her failure.

They have an unplanned audience, too.

Though it's midnight and most stores are closed, residents scurry home along sidewalks carrying bags and wrapped gifts no doubt from Macy's, Barnes & Noble, Bloomingdales and more, wrapped in winter coats as they watch, freezing, in the snow. Traffic jams the block with people travelling home for Christmas to be with their families—all typical in the city that never sleeps.

Nobody cares, though.

Nobody cries.

And why should they, when their own lives are, in comparison, so unrealised?

Noah Finn & the Art of Conception

It haunts their faces; their voices mere echoes in the distance as Noah creates an alternate universe, cast out along another temporary time-line.

And it's all for you, Maria.

As a child, she stole Marshal's toys.

As a teen, she stole the spotlight.

Now, as an adult, Maria has stolen Marshal's future.

But she can no longer steal from him.

Though every fibre of her being yearns for the day to reset itself and for Noah to have mercy, her soul heaves a sigh of relief.

It worked.

From now on, Marshal is free.

Free of her.

Free of this world.

Forever.

Chapter Two
DEATH WANTS A WORD

Noah waits until the ambulance carrying Marshal's body is out of sight, then starts his meeting with Maria by placing a hand on her sweat-soaked forehead. Through his energy, he breathes into her temporary life—it's faint and fragile, but valuable.

There's a building excitement Maria recognises, reflecting the carefree, upbeat woman she once was. A woman who never failed to put on her make-up or style her hair. One who wore a constant smile even when her luck initially took a turn for the worst—an empathetic, kind soul.

***

Maria startles awake, screaming and cursing

and scrambling to feel for her legs. She's hyperventilating, grateful this entire ordeal was only a nightmare. She's standing beside her parked car, dressed as if arriving home from the office. It's eerily quiet on the Upper East Side, but the tranquillity and elegance of its tree-lined streets and proximity to Central Park was part of the reason she and Marshal chose to live here.

Although the key is still in the ignition, the engine and the lights are off and she's alone in the dark.

She rummages in her handbag for her door keys.

Her watch reads 9 pm.

Little does she know her time is almost up.

Noah stands beneath a streetlight and gently waves her over as she heads for the front door. Maria pauses and frowns, trying to remember if she knows this man—is he a neighbour, or a bum passing through?

She rummages a little faster, deeper.

She hears her keys jingling somewhere amongst the junk at the bottom and sticks her head in to get a better view. When she looks up, she and Noah are face-to-face. He's blocking the path to the steps leading to her large wooden front door.

"The least you could do is wave back." He tuts.

Maria drops her handbag and squeaks, clapping a hand to her chest.

Her heart rate remains the same.

"Don't hurt me. Take what you want."

Noah raises his palms and frowns. "I won't, Maria; you have nothing I want."

"My phone and purse are in there. Just take them and go. I won't call 9-1-1."

"You can't if I take your phone, silly," says Noah, scratching his chin, "or at all now, come to think of it."

Maria peers around his pale, blonde head, judging the distance between the car and the safety of her home. As he steps out of the shadows, Maria sees he's wearing a black suit and in his top pocket is a blue handkerchief— old, torn and fading. His shirt is white, splattered red at the cuffs.

"And how do you know my name?" Maria retorts. She realises her keys are in the bag at her feet. "Marshal, come out here, I need help!"

"He's gone," Noah tells her, "and he's not coming back."

"Who are you? What do you want?"

"I want to help you," he replies, reaching to scoop up the handbag and the escaped contents, including a rose lipstick, a comb and her precious keys. "Can we talk?"

"What's with the suit?"

"I'm in mourning. Someone died," he tells her, only half-lying.

Maria shakes her head. "I'm sorry. Who are you, again?"

"I'm here to give you some grim news." Noah offers her the bag and its contents, including her keys. "Could we go inside?"

"If you're a cop, where's your badge?" Maria hesitates and raises her brow, then reaches out to take her possessions. "Got any ID?"

"I don't, I'm afraid. My name is Noah and my responsibilities are deeper than law enforcement."

"So, you're with the government?"

He extends a hand. "Sorry I scared you."

Glaring at the bloodstains, Maria tentatively accepts the shake.

"What happened?"

"It's not my blood," he assures her. "I really *must* talk to you as a matter of urgency. We're against the clock."

Chapter Three
CAN I COME IN?

"May we talk inside, please?" Noah asks again.

Indecisive for a further few seconds, Maria eases towards her door, overtaking Noah as she does so and turning her back to him. She fumbles to find the correct key on her chain before finally agreeing to let him in.

"Can I get you something to drink?" she asks.

It takes Noah a few moments to respond, causing him to feel foolish and a little more human than he's accustomed to. His authentic form is incapable of consuming anything at all. He tried once in the company of a previous client, Andrew Law, and terrified them both. If Andrew wasn't already dead and on his way to a well-deserved afterlife, Noah was sure he'd have had a heart attack.

Noah Finn & the Art of Conception

Distracted by the eccentricity of Maria and Marshal's home, Noah is in awe of the vibrantly painted walls in purples, oranges and yellows. He expected to see art strewn in every room and elegant décor; instead, he finds speckled carpets and wacky, patterned curtains. It all screams love and light, laughter and life.

"What a lovely home," he exaggerates, ignoring her offer of a beverage because he can't drink it, anyway. "Take a seat."

"Alright," Maria says, gesturing for him to do the same.

Noah is usually only responsible for a client's afterlife, not the events leading to it. He'll have a *lot* of explaining to do at 'head office' for Maria's case, though he's here with his boss's permission... *sort of.*

He adjusts his suit and perches on the edge of a purple sofa opposite Maria's chair. It creaks beneath his weight, which he imagines (given the unfortunate news he's about to share), is twice his regular size today. Being what he is, he stifles a grin; no matter the circumstances, he cannot truly weigh *anything,* not how humans perceive it. To Noah, it's often like he is physically carrying his client's pain and grief until he's able to guide them safely through the other side. The weight of responsibility lifts for a while, but it's not long until he's under pressure again.

"I'm afraid I have some uncomfortable news about your brother, Marshal."

The blood drains from Maria's face as she reads between the lines. This stranger is here to tell her she'll never see him again—not breathing, anyway.

Moments ago, she called Marshal's name and asked for his help, getting no response. Why didn't she realise sooner and spare herself this embarrassment?

Only now does she register how late it is and wonder why she's unable to recall where she's been or what she was doing before being intercepted. She doesn't even remember which route she took home from work.

Maria swallows hard.

Her throat is dry. Her palms are sweating.

What's wrong with me?

"Is he alive?"

Noah pauses and looks down at his hands—steady and interlocked, as always.

"I'm sorry," he replies, "but Marshal died tonight in a car accident. Although this is a tragedy, it's not the message I'm here to deliver."

There's a pounding in Maria's ears and a drumming in her chest; an internal orchestra deafening her with adrenaline and panic. Her fingers are shaking now, tingling as the blood rushes to prepare her to fight or flee as far from this situation as possible.

Dead? she thinks. *How can he be dead? I saw him this morning!*

"Flight won't help," Noah tells her. "It won't change anything."

"How did you—"

Maria hears what sounds like metal grinding against metal and a man yelling orders amidst a wailing siren. She tilts her head, confused by the flood of unexplained noise, and jumps up to shake off what she assumes is a hallucination—a sensation caused by the firing chemical reactions in her brain, helping an already stressed body to cope with losing a loved one.

"I feel sick."

She hurries to the window and flings it open, hoping to catch a breath of fresh air. In the street, the emergency services are working on a small green car, half-crumpled against a lamppost in deep snow and rear-ended by a grey pickup truck. There is glass and debris scattered across the sidewalk and blood splattered against the passenger window.

As she turns to tell Noah—to ask if he sees it too—she startles. He's already beside her, holding back the curtain to allow them both an unobstructed view.

"A tragic accident," he explains. "One dead. One in a coma. The other paralysed. Three lives changed in the blink of an eye; a decision made by one selfish woman in less than a second has affected not only hers, but her brother's and a stranger's lives forever."

He places a familiar hand on her shoulder, jolting Maria through her confusion and back into the world. Violent images bombard her head, blood and broken glass decorate her clothing and the steering wheel. She hears, much clearer now, the crunching of the car's bonnet as it slams into the post, throwing both occupants toward the dashboard, then against the windows. The fireman's calming voice surrounds her as he leans across the wheel to cut through her seatbelt.

A steadily playing violin is their soundtrack.

The little car is her own. That frightened driver is strikingly familiar—same wild blonde hair and matching attire.

Wait, is that me?

Marshal is slumped across the dashboard with his eyes wide and mouth agape; an expression capturing, in a mortifying snapshot, the horror of his death.

Noah Finn & the Art of Conception

The helicopter about to land will take Maria and the stranger from the truck to the hospital where she will only spend a few days, but he will spend countless, meaningless years. Maria wonders where in the street it could land. The situation really *must* be dire.

"His name is Emmanuel Mirh," Noah tells her and releases Maria's shoulder.

She gasps as she finds herself stood on the sidewalk again, staring at her front door as if nothing happened.

The key is in the ignition.

But this time, the headlights are on.

Chapter Four
HELLO, MARIA

Though she still cannot feel her heart racing, with a tight chest and quaking hands, Maria jumps into the car and slams the door. She reaches out and grips the wheel, attempting to ground herself. Outside, snow is gently falling, and flakes now sit in her golden hair like tiny diamonds. There's no other traffic on the street or neighbours snooping from their windows; the atmosphere is still... empty.

Maria is sitting in a void or a vacuum with only her breathing, paranoid thoughts and confusion to backfill it.

"Hello again, Maria."

Maria screams. *There's someone in the car!*

She throws the door open and collapses across the sidewalk, crawling for the front door on her drenched hands and knees. Her grey dress drags across the frozen path. Her knees scrape against stone, but they don't bleed.

"Where are you going?"

"I must be dreaming. I'm dreaming!"

"You're not dreaming. Come back."

Noah snaps his fingers and Maria is suddenly sitting in the driver's seat again, dumbfounded. Her mouth hangs agape, and she's not only hyperventilating, but shaking her head rapidly from side-to-side to wake up or, as she hopes, snap back to reality.

"You're not dreaming," he repeats. "I'm sorry but your brother *is* dead and you're in a *lot* of trouble. Do you have any idea how much you have inconvenienced my boss? The big man's pissed off. And considering punishing you. I convinced him to wait before he decides on your options; I think if we were to spend some time together, you'd soon acknowledge the error of your ways and apologise for your sins... or what you humans understand as sins, anyway."

"What are you talking about? What sins?"

Noah ignores her. "I have a future in mind for you, Maria, but *I'm* not the one you have to convince. You're in denial and that's normal. Take your time, I'm not going anywhere."

Maria makes a break for her front door again, catching Noah a little off guard, but it's nothing he can't handle. He rolls his eyes and clicks his fingers and Maria is back in the car... again. Sweating this time, but much less disturbed by the event as if she expected it.

"I can do this all night, all week, all month, all year... pretty much for as long as this world is in existence, Maria. Hopefully, we won't have to because the clock is ticking." He taps his wrist where a watch would be. "Eventually, you'll accept me."

"Accept you?" She gulps down her air, then wipes her forehead on the rim of her dress. Only now does she notice the rip in her thick winter tights. "Who, or should I ask *what* the hell are you? No lies!"

"I never lied to you."

"You said you worked for the government."

"No," he says, grinning, "*you* said I worked for the government, I just didn't disagree. And who lets a strange man into their home with no credentials and turns her back to him? I mean, *really*, Maria! You were practically asking to die—good job I'm not a murderer because with an attitude like yours, it wouldn't have been long."

Maria raises her hands in surrender, then covers her face and utters, "I'm dead?"

Noah shrugs. "Sort of. I paused your existence along a temporary timeline. Time doesn't exist here, but the sooner you can transition the better."

"Transition to where? I don't understand, I was on my way home from work and then—"

"Ah yes, your unfulfilling work; potentially one of the many reasons we're in this situation. But let's not blame others for our mistakes." Noah clears his throat. "You were in the car with Marshal when you made a very poor decision. Now, you're in what I guess some religions refer to as Limbo until my boss can decide what to do with you based on my report."

"Who is your boss?"

"God."

"God?"

"Well, not really because God doesn't exist. But universal energy does, though it's all the same thing underneath the labels and segregation. I'm part of that energy."

Maria is speechless.

Noah chuckles. "I didn't get it at first, either. I call him Christopher Saint; he is everything and everyone. I'm one of Christopher's employees. I'm a reaper, and it's my job to deal with the aftermath of stupid human decisions like yours. This tragic incident, though, requires a little more work. Christopher wanted you to live, but you wanted to die. Christopher wonders if I can get through to you. So, Hi! I'm Noah."

"You're the Grim Reaper then?" Maria asks, still unconvinced this isn't just a nightmare or her brother's idea of a practical joke.

"You could say that. To make matters worse, though, you wanted to take another two lives with you against their will today, which raised some red flags. We can't have that, I'm afraid. Messes with the system. Messes with the plan."

"System? Plan?"

"Mmm-hmm. So I'm here to teach you some important lessons, Maria, and you'll learn them. Where you're going, *hopefully*, you'll need them."

"But, what if I can't?"

Noah cracks his knuckles for effect. "Can't or won't? Not only will your brother die, but Emmanuel will die and *you* will die. Three lives for the price of one. We don't get that kind of deal every day." He winks.

"Then I did you a favour, even if I don't remember doing anything, crashing my car or how I got here. Why would I kill myself or my brother? I love my brother!"

"Dunno, you tell me."

"I can't. I don't remember."

"Better think," says Noah, "because death comes to us all, Maria, and it hasn't *quite* gotten round to you yet. If I were you, I'd start running."

Chapter Five
RUN FOR YOUR FUTURE

She may not be able to run away from this nightmare, but Maria knows she can run from Noah. She takes off in the opposite direction, back towards where, in her mind, the park would normally be. Towards people.

After five minutes she wonders why she isn't out of breath or why her ankles aren't aching. Her limbs aren't cold from the night air, either.

After ten minutes, she sees a familiar house appear on the right-hand side.

Her house.

Maria spins and starts running, but after a short while, there's her house again. She collapses in the road, unafraid of being hit by a passing vehicle because there are none, and she expects in this universe there will be none. Since arriving, she's seen nobody else at all (except for Death, or so he claims to be). On her knees and trying her hardest not to cry, Maria gives in and relaxes, letting the snow slowly blanket her.

This is a staging area, she realises, designed to mimic her life for comfort and reassurance as she learns to accept Noah's message.

"Alright, I'm listening," she sobs. "I can't run from this. I want to go home!"

Maria's bottom lip quivers as a firm hand squeezes her shoulder. When she looks up through sapphire-coloured, tear-filled eyes, she sees Noah's dazzling blue staring back at her. His warm blonde hair glows in the moonlight. Maria feels comforted and ready to accept whatever he has in store.

Be it life or death, she no longer cares.

"Acceptance *is* hard," he tells her, agreeing such a reaction is normal and perfectly understandable. "Gets easier, but the truth never leaves you."

"I killed my brother, that man Mr Mirh and perhaps myself? That's the truth?"

"Yes," Noah says, "that's the truth."

Maria sniffles and wipes her nose with the back of her hand. "Can you fix it?"

"No."

She nods. "Can *I* fix it?"

"Maybe."

"So help me," she says. "I won't run anymore, I promise."

Noah offers his hand and hauls her up, then dusts down her dress with his palm. She watches him quizzically, baffled by how much care and love she sees in this fantastical being.

Though he looks and sounds like a person, she senses he's something extreme and incomprehensible beneath the friendly facet.

"I was human once," he says, taking Maria by surprise. "Oh no, I can't read your mind—not fully. I sense your confusion and see how you're studying me. Don't be frightened. I can't hurt you; taking people isn't my job."

"Death's job is to take people to their afterlife."

"I'm not the one who kills you. I just deal with the aftermath, transportation, and help you understand the circumstances—your transition. Your ultimate destination is your choice."

"But, you're hoping I'll go somewhere specific?"

He nods and gestures for Maria to join him. The two begin a steady stroll back to the car.

"Just over 22 years ago I was in your position. Tired with living, working a job I hated, planning my death and failing. Never tried to take anyone else with me, but I did... in a way. The people *I* extinguished were still living. Their grief for me almost swallowed them whole, and that's when Christopher intervened. He helped me see my mistakes and comprehend how important forgiveness is. It's all the same. Everything is one, but not necessarily whole."

"Why are *you* helping me? Why not Christopher?"

"With my help, I intend to pay Christopher's kindness forward and prove you're right for the afterlife I have planned for you. When I tell you my story, I'm hoping you can better judge your actions. But first," he says, sighing, "let's see how you're coping right now."

Chapter Six
HELP ARRIVES

Noah gives Maria a firm shove as she approaches her front door. She tenses, expecting to smack her head on the step. Instead of falling on top, Maria's body melts through and out the other side.

She's back at the scene of the accident, wincing as the pain of her many injuries reminds her that for now, she is still alive. It's so different from being in Limbo where pain is dull—her body almost numb and her heartbeat on pause. Now, the metal traps her legs, her neck and head are throbbing and warm blood is trickling from a gash across her forehead. Her matted hair is blood-soaked, and she has stabbing pains down both arms from bracing at impact.

Noah Finn & the Art of Conception

For now, the post she hit appears sturdy.

She never thought she'd pray to a God, but as she's glaring through her spider-web windscreen, she prays it remains upright.

There are flashing lights and sirens surrounding the vehicle but as they've not yet removed Marshal from the passenger side, she focuses on one of them in particular to distract her grief.

His face displays a gentle smile; he's sympathetic and trying to keep her attention while someone in a different uniform—a fireman because of the red and yellow—cuts through the roof.

Someone leans in to support her head in his hands; the touch is soothing. Their face is a blur, but at least someone cares.

She's not alone.

And although there are lots of other people at the scene, some trying to help the car behind, it is Noah's presence in the back of her mind that registers.

"Miss Shephard, can you still hear me?" asks a male voice.

When she doesn't respond, he shouts, "Maria, stay awake!"

He tells her to be as still as she can and that she shouldn't doze off.

Stay awake.
Stay alive.

A stranger crouches by her side until they're ready to remove her from the wreckage. He warns she may feel some discomfort. She doubts it—she'll most likely pass out again and, comprehending the severity of their situation, she prays for that, too.

She hopes to see Noah again.

At the edge of Maria's peripheral vision, faces are appearing to get a better look at the accident, hoping to see something gruesome and social media worthy. There are camera phones, media vans and other passers-by stopping to gawk at her misfortune, and when someone pulls a body bag from the back of the ambulance to house Marshal's corpse, a few even shout and whoop.

Are their minds so filled with petty problems like last-minute Christmas bargains to really *see* her; see her the way humans *should* see one another?

There's a helicopter approaching, too. She can hear it, though she has no way of knowing if it's to film or save her.

A fleeting thought passes through her distracted brain—*I wonder what it's like to fly.*

Then she wants to scream at everyone, hit

them and call them obscene names again.

Years of violent movies, TV shows and video games have brainwashed them that this behaviour is acceptable. Before the end of the day, her story will have gone viral with harsh comments, thumbs up emoticons and other outrageous reactions. Most likely, her friends and family will hear about what happened through the internet before the emergency services can call them.

Amongst the vehicles surrounding the scene are three Police cars—two guarding the block to prevent anyone passing and one on standby to follow the ambulance to the hospital. Should she regain consciousness enough to explain, they will interview and question her about Marshal's death there.

What was going through her mind on impact?
I wanted to die.

Did she lose control or swerve purposefully?
Yes.

Is she on any medication for depression or anxiety?
Yes.

Has she had any thoughts of suicide and self-

harm?
Hell, yes.

Was she aware her brother, Marshal, was dead?
I am now.

What did she have to say for herself?
Fuck all!

She will have the right to an attorney and they may even handcuff her to the bed, though being paralysed, she won't get very far without being seen.

Her predicament is clear.

Maria will spend the rest of her life in a prison be it physically, mentally or emotionally; her punishment for killing two people and attempting suicide will never end.

Maria closes her eyes.

Punish me. I'm ready.

Chapter Seven
HERE'S WHAT HAPPENED

"I hear you," Noah says and clambers into the passenger side of her car.

He slams the door to keep out the night air. The cold may not bother Maria here, but he wants her completely focused on the conversation inside.

"Tell me, why did you want to die today?"

"I've wanted to die for the past six months," she replies, twiddling the hem of her dress between her fingers. "And I didn't *really* want to die at all. Earlier this year, I went to the doctor for some checks. My boyfriend Joey and I were struggling to conceive, and I expected them to tell me not to worry—everything's fine. Then, to be meeting a friend for coffee 20 minutes later."

"They found Cancer?"

Maria shakes her head. "Sometimes I wish they did, then maybe I'd have a chance."

It wasn't Cancer. Noah already knows. But he wants her to admit the problem; to explain why she feels the way she does. Like a failure: less of a woman, a disappointment, a waste of Joey's time.

"They told me I couldn't have children. My boyfriend was distraught. He's older than me and always wanted kids. Because I couldn't provide, we parted ways."

"We?"

"No," she says and dabs her eyes. "*He* left *me*. And I understood. I have no right to ask him to give up his future for me. I'm better paired with someone like me or someone who doesn't need children to be complete."

"You're incomplete?"

Maria rubs her shoulders and tenses as the cold begins to seep into her bones.

Noah smiles.

His plan is working.

"I didn't at first. I assumed we'd find some other way. But he wanted natural, biological children."

"Why?"

"It's how he always pictured his life. Two kids, a dog, a house with a picket fence and corporate jobs. Eventually. But, I spilt red paint across his pretty picture. Now I'm worthless. Tarnished or broken or something." She watches her breath float across the steering wheel and slowly fade. "Why can I suddenly feel, Noah?"

He winks. "You're *allowing* yourself to. You still have a lot to offer someone who deserves you. Flashy job. Good looks."

Maria furiously rubs her arms. She's freezing. "What use am I? At that moment, my unfulfilled purpose defined me—I will never be a mother. No matter who I meet, I will always have to survive the inevitable disclosure and watch them walk away."

"Not necessarily," Noah tells her, "because you said yourself not all men want or can have children."

"And how long would it take me to find someone I bonded with who fit my criteria? What, am I supposed to hand out a questionnaire?"

"You *know* that's not how this works."

"I'll spend the rest of my life alone, I realised. I just can't."

"So, you thought about killing yourself," Noah says.

"I decided I didn't want to live. There's a sizeable difference."

"Yet the outcome is the same. You no longer physically exist in the lives of your loving parents, brother, colleagues or friends. You're gone forever, and leave them behind to grieve, only their memories of you intact."

Maria feels a twang of pain in her left wrist as she reaches over to take Noah's hand. She imagines it's the ghost of what's happening in reality; as she lets Noah in, her body lets in the pain. Perhaps the EMTs are finally moving her.

"You're mostly pain-free for now," Noah tells her as she twists her wrist in a smooth, slow circle. "But the more you progress and accept your fate, the more alive and therefore in pain you will be. Pain is life."

"I disagree," she utters, shaking her head. "Life is not pain. Life should be happiness and joy and love and family. It should be hope."

"I said that pain is life, Maria, not life is pain."

"Same thing," she utters.

"Absolutely not. Pain is a part of life, Maria, and every living thing that exists in this universe experiences pain at some point. Some more than others, granted, and these are the tragedies like yours. There are also people worse off, which is why gratitude is life, too."

Maria ponders silently. Sure, everyone feels pain at some point—it's difficult going through life without stubbing your toe or getting a headache. Few will experience the psychological torture of *her* pain in the way she does.

And if they had to spend but 30 seconds in her brain, they too would wish for death.

"Pain has a direct line to the heart, Maria. Physical symptoms don't define pain. It's interwoven in our psyche; expressed and shared in endless ways. Pain prompts emotional responses; few human beings truly understand that."

"And you understand pain, do you?" Maria asks bitterly.

Noah smiles. "I think it's time I told you how I died—I, too, once hoped to fly."

Chapter Eight
NOAH'S STORY

Noah takes Maria to the top of a skyscraper; it's choking, a claustrophobic scene from his past. Even if Maria wasn't afraid of heights or uncomfortable standing so close to the edge, given her desire to die, she'd *still* hate every second of this experience.

He holds Maria back as she watches a young man in overalls step over the railing and dangle outward, closing his eyes and preparing to jump —*to fly*. Her feet urge her forward because she recognises the body shape, hair colour and height of the man.

It's a snapshot of Noah Finn's last moments on Earth.

"Wait!" she yells, hoping he'll hear her.

To her left, Noah giggles. "It already

happened, Maria, there's nothing you can do."

Merely seconds later, in the distance, Maria and Noah see a low-flying aeroplane heading for the building. Past Noah leaps back over the railing and sets off running toward them. A plume of smoke consumes him as he's thrown over the edge. Maria feels the debris and smog clog her lungs and the lurch of the building's foundations as she, too, falls after him.

Her body and Noah's spirit connect for a second in a strange, distant way. Like family.

The scene is fast-forwarded. Now safe from harm, Noah and Maria sit beside a pair of shoes sticking up through the rubble on a roof somewhere in the city. A church, maybe. She grounds herself, using both hands to ensure the surface beneath is firm and her vision is no longer spinning.

Then it hits her.

Maria glares, dumbfounded. "I remember this. They found a man at St. Paul's on 9/11. You died in the terrorist attack and landed in the shape of a cross. I can't believe it's *you!*"

How can such an inspirational symbol for faith and togetherness have died so horribly and be facing death and anguish daily?

"I chose my fate," he says, "to help

Christopher find someone who could do the job I turned down. But that's not why I brought you here."

"Why did you?"

"Because, no matter how sorry for yourself you are, there are *always* people suffering harder, for longer and in more tragic circumstances." He holds up his hands. "I'm not denying your circumstances aren't tragic. They are 100 percent. If they existed for this, you'd be winning awards. But they don't, and you're not."

He nods, satisfied.

Maria shuffles uncomfortably atop the debris, trying not to look at Past Noah's shoes.

"Does visiting this place upset you?" she asks, brow raised.

"I bring lots of clients here. It helps put things in perspective."

"It's so depressing, though."

"We cannot change the past, Maria. I could have gone home, but I repaid Christopher's kindness instead. I help more people in this role than I would have in the one Christopher hoped I'd take."

"Which was what?"

Noah laughs. "I'll get to it. Everyone receives different options, and it's up to that person to reflect on what they've learned to choose the best afterlife. You'll get a few when we part ways. Some will seem selfish, others selfless. Your path is your own. Until then, perhaps turn your attention to the future, or the past—both, I guess!"

"You're insane and you're confusing me. *Why* did you bring me here, Noah? To brag that you're a famous corpse? What does *any* of this have to do with *my* accident?"

"We're all insane in a world where insanity is sanity," Noah says. "It has everything to do with your accident. I want to show how when we commit suicide—though it turns out I didn't, the disaster killed me—we can still complete a selfless, helpful act to save others in our final moments and often, we do this naturally because it's how our souls reach out."

"Through the options we choose? My soul isn't dead yet, Noah, and I didn't commit suicide. *I'm* a murderer."

"True, but you still hope for death. Remember those red flags I talked about? The universe selected you today. It all started with your craving for suicide, for silence, then your stupidity on a symbolic evening. You and I are much the same, I'm afraid."

She tuts. "We're nothing alike."

"I disagree. When we die, we leave others behind. Like your parents who watched you grow into the woman you are today. Like your friends who share your passions and your hobbies. Like your pets who rely so heavily on you. You have two dogs, right?"

Maria's eyes widen. "All knowing?"

"Precisely. Protect these connections in any way we can. It's not *their* fault you'd prefer silence to their company. You and I both did."

"That's not why I wanted to die, Noah. They can take care of themselves. They have each other to lean on. Their lives are not my responsibility. They wouldn't expect me to worry so heavily about them when I have an afterlife to select, just as I would not wish to burden them, either."

"Your life *is* your parents' responsibility because they *created* you. You blame people in your life for your unhappiness, don't you?"

"The only person I blame is myself and, for leaving me, Joey. And my parents did not create me. Marshal and I are both adopted—he and I aren't even blood relatives! I know little about my mother, only she struggled to cope and my birth added to complex circumstances. I've never needed to search further. I love the family I have."

"And Joey?"

"I understand why he left and I wouldn't suggest he's responsible for my outlook on life.

It is what it is. I'd have come to the same conclusion eventually if we got married, anyway."

"So with or without your desired outcome, you'd be opting out?" Noah sighs.

"That's not what I said! He wasn't my desired outcome."

"Wow, you're *really* in denial, aren't you?" Noah exhales deeply and wrings his hands together. "I blamed my ex too for my unhappiness, but I still became a symbol of community and love on a day when there was little faith in anything—when all the world saw was hatred and violence. *And* we made friends again, even in death. Maria, I have a limited amount of time to prove you deserve a second chance and that, wherever life leads, you can make up for your foolishness. The universe flagged your dying light for a reason; it's expecting redemption."

"I never asked for your help, Noah. I never asked you to represent me."

"Would you rather I leave?"

Maria groans, unsure what she wants. "How can one tiny kind act make *any* difference?" she asks, sceptically. "It's not as simple as that. I expressed love and kindness every day before my accident and even more so when I learned I would never carry a child of my own. I reached out, people reached back, and we cared for one another in a support group. It didn't work. I'm still here. The other women in my position are *still* grieving over what they can never have. *We're* still having this conversation."

"What are you saying?"

"Redemption doesn't matter. I'm saying that sometimes our actions fade with the wind, Noah, and that's OK."

"You're wrong. Your act becomes another's inspiration to act, which becomes an act, and it goes on and on and on until *someone*, *somewhere*, benefits. You may not have seen it, but you changed so many lives by attending that support group. What we need to show Christopher is how you will pay this forward the way I repaid his kindness. The universe chose me for a reason, too. Do you think you can get your head out of your ass long enough to indulge me? What the *hell* else have you got to do that's so pressing?"

Maria scowls, then shrugs. "There's no need to be rude. You're more of an asshole than they made you out to be on TV."

PART TWO

The Visitors

Chapter Nine
LOSING MY MIND

It's still 11:59 pm.
With one swish of his hand, Noah deletes the scene on the road as if Maria's accident never happened. In its place, with a flick of the other, he re-creates an argument she had with Marshal the day before.

"Tell me," Noah prompts, "what's going on here?"

Already fragile and losing control of her emotions, she's animated and red in the face.

Why doesn't Marshal ever listen to her?

Why must they always do things *his* way?

"We were talking about my parents," she says in a whisper.

"Looks to me like *you* were shouting and Marshal was tolerating it."

"I'm not proud," she confesses, "but I'm not

sorry, either. He wouldn't listen."

"What were you arguing over, Christmas gifts?"

"No, my mother's care."

"What about it specifically?"

"She has Dementia, if you must know."

"I already do but you must talk about your troubles aloud."

Maria grunts. "I tried. He wasn't willing to accept she may need to be in a care home—this will be her last Christmas at the house with Dad. She needs trained professionals capable of dealing with her illness and making her more comfortable."

Noah nods. "You wanted to take a tour of two nursing homes nearby, right?"

"I wanted to find somewhere safe, cheerful and close to the family. We'd still see her every day, but we wouldn't have to fret over her losing things, wandering off or hurting herself. She was forgetting to turn off the stove or lock the door. She almost poured boiling kettle water over her hands, trying to wash soap from them! Marshal caught her just in time, but he didn't register how severe it could get or the potential outcomes. I couldn't bear to see it. She's my mum!"

Maria begins to cry and Noah hands her the tatty blue handkerchief from his pocket, which she thanks him for and blows into.

"Alzheimer's is a cruel disease," Noah agrees.

"We should have realised sooner. But, you don't always register how silly forgetful moments could be something more sinister."

He nods. "And why *would* you just assume the worst? Old age and memory problems go hand-in-hand."

"Exactly," Maria says. "My dad's is still intact and fully functioning, but his physical strength isn't what it once was. Something else old age brings. He's been labelling things and setting alarms for my mum. Marshal couldn't face that, either. We all used to go fishing together, play card games and have picnics in the park, sipping flasks of coffee and chomping on biscuits. There are so many holiday traditions we're breaking this year because Mum and Dad aren't up for them."

Maria explains how her dad gets tired quickly, needs a cane to walk further than the garden gate and doesn't have the strength to reel in a fish or the co-ordination to drive a car any longer. He can't get to the drug store to collect medication. He can't haul the grocery shopping.

Having made his peace with the situation, accepting he's getting older, he frequently jokes about it.

"We all get old and die eventually," he once

told Maria, thankfully not in the presence of her brother. They adopted both their children late in life but never regretted it. "When it's my time, I'll go willingly and gracefully. None of this hair dye, Botox, butt-lifting shit they show on the television!"

Maria laughs at that memory and hopes her parents can make it to the hospital to visit if Noah and Christopher allow her to live; to hold them both tightly again and kiss their cheeks, see their smiling faces, and grasp their hands would be a blessing and enough for her.

It would be enough for them.

"She's fading away," she tells Noah, "and my heart is fading with her. Around a week ago, I sat to watch television with her in the living room. She likes documentaries about animals and nature, wonders of the world. I heard a crunch and pulled a half-eaten digestive biscuit from the back of the cushion. Something I've been seeing a lot of lately—abandoned plates of food, half-finished chores. She'll put down her tea and forget, then have to pour another. Dad said he's watching her closely in the kitchen with cutlery, pots and pans, cleaning chemicals, afraid she'll drink something she shouldn't or slice her finger. He constantly has to babysit— monitor her behaviour, any declines in physical or mental health. In return, he's suffering, too."

"We'll do anything for the people we love, Maria. Your brother saw what you see; he may just have had a harder time accepting what it meant for his future."

"I think he couldn't accept what it meant for *theirs*. That hurt him more."

Noah nods and rewinds the scene in the street, taking Maria's life back another 48 hours to a breakdown in her car in the parking lot of her friend's workplace. She'd agreed to collect Angela and take her out grocery shopping until they returned her car from the garage later that day.

She'd arrived early, alone with her thoughts.

"And how about here?" Noah asks. "Explain your feelings."

"I can't." She dries more falling tears from the end of her nose and chin. "I got thinking about my parents and my ex-boyfriend and what I can never have. Depression, I guess, because it was all happening so suddenly."

In the car, the past Maria leans her head against the steering wheel, turning off the ignition, and heaves with sorrow. She hammers her forehead against the leather a few times, honking the horn at least twice by mistake, then slumps and screams.

Thankfully, nobody sees her outburst.

Maria watches herself pitifully. "I just wanted the negative thoughts to stop but no matter what I found to raise my spirits, something always ruined it."

"Can you give me an example?" Noah snaps his fingers to dry the handkerchief, so it's fresh for Maria to continue using. "When did you find something happy that turned out to be sad?"

"Two weeks ago, my aunt called and said she'd be flying over from the UK to spend Christmas with us this year."

"That's lovely news," Noah agrees. "She arrived safely?"

"Yes, she's here. I mean, she was. I mean... how does time work in this bloody place?" She sighs. "It elated me; we haven't seen Aunt Becca in six years. Neither our side nor hers could afford the flights until now."

"What went so wrong about that?"

"I realised it would be the last time we all spent Christmas together as a family. Soon my mother will die, her sister will probably die back in England before her next visit, and suddenly I had assigned myself the immense responsibility of making this holiday the best and most significant in our history because it would be so meaningful."

"That is a *tremendous* responsibility, Maria, and something one individual shouldn't bare."

"You're telling me!"

"It's a burden you started alone, though, and ultimately you must have seen that because you bailed. Did you invite your family to help or express these thoughts to anyone else?"

"I'd upset or worry them. I couldn't bring them down or ask them to do more than they already have. At the moment, my dad's sister, Marshal and I manage Mum's care. My dad, too, when he's well enough. They're on call 24-7."

"As are you, mentally."

Maria scowls. "How do you work *that* out?"

"Even now, unconscious and bleeding in the helicopter, you're thinking not of yourself but of your mother and how grateful you are for her care. Gratitude is your biggest step, Maria. Appreciating what we have can sometimes be difficult, however small things are. Family is usually first on the list. It was for me."

"And how about for Christopher? What was on *his* gratitude list?"

"I couldn't tell you. He was the first to take another life, though, so I guess he was grateful for mercy when he didn't go straight to Hell, even though it doesn't *technically* exist. Which is why he's in the position he's in. You'd have to ask Christopher because I wouldn't want to pry. It's too personal."

"Then why should *I*?"

"Because you have something in common he and I don't."

"Which is?"

"You're both murderers," he says, "but you're both sorry... *right*?"

Chapter Ten
THERE IS NO HELL

"What do you *mean* there is no Hell?" Maria asks, taken aback by his bold statement.

"Hell is a label you humans apply to suffer through the options you originally chose, then regretted choosing," Noah explains. "Just as there is no Heaven, God, angels or anything else like marriage, birth, death and so on."

"There's no such thing as getting married or being born or dying? I have to disagree, Noah," Maria says. "You're denying three things almost *every* human being on the planet goes through. To announce it's all fiction?"

"It exists, just not individually. It's part of the bigger picture... the universe. It's part of Christopher, and Christopher simply is."

"Is what?"

"He just *is*. I appreciate you probably want to

punch me, but I can't explain any further than I already have. Labels aside, if you're alive, you're probably taking part in rituals developed by religions or cults or governments to help you comprehend that the world around you is, in fact, incomprehensible. Like Christmas."

"If I try any harder to wrap my tiny human brain around the concept, I'll implode. Are you're trying to tell me human beings create realities and live by their own rules because that's not what the original design looks like?"

"Correct." Noah smiles and claps his hands. "*Now* we're getting somewhere! But listen, I need you to explain something."

Maria raises her brow. "Uh, sure."

"Why do you hate Christmas?"

Maria startles. "I love Christmas, what are you talking about?"

"You ended your life on Christmas Eve?"

"I don't think the date even registered."

Noah winks. "More than you know."

Noah clicks his fingers again and Maria is sitting in the car with her brother, Marshal. She recognises the clothing she's wearing in the scene because she's wearing it now—a grey dress, tights and a headband. By the looks of their surroundings and the fact Marshal is breathing (even if he's crying), it's around an hour before Maria made that heart-wrenching decision to kill them both. 10 pm, maybe.

"Why is Marshal crying?" Noah asks, leading her toward the driver's window to better hear the conversation inside. "Until today, had you ever seen him cry?"

Maria can't help but turn away, struggling to look Marshal in the eye.

He's focused on Maria's face and is scowling as she explains what her plan is and how she can 'help' them both through their suffering. Marshal is shaking his head and refusing, arguing, and he tries to get out of the car. He would rather walk to the nearest Police station than listen to this shit or call Maria's doctor to report her mindset. Not only is Maria threatening to end her life, but she's offering to help end his... and on Christmas Eve!

"Why do you turn away?" Noah asks, nudging her shoulder with his. "Can't take your own actions?"

"No, I can take them," she snaps. "I'm just not sorry for them."

"That's why you're turning away? You're glad Marshal's dead?"

"I'm not glad he's dead!" she bites, yanking her shoulder back and ambling from the car. "You don't get it. He didn't understand what the future had in store for him and I wanted to protect him; I wanted us to be together, to be free."

"Free of what?"

"Of this!" Maria holds out her arms and spins, kicking up the snow to create a cloud of fine white fog. "This world. This existence. It's painful. It's filled with sorrow and unfair outcomes!"

"Such as your inability to have a child? Why not adopt as your parents did."

"Don't you think I would have if Joey agreed? And Marshal, he—" Her voice breaks. "He has—*had?*—Cancer. He'd have died not long after my mother, even after undergoing chemo. Reminded through one final Christmas of his suffering. It's *cruel*."

Noah lowers his voice. "I'm sorry."

"You should be! This is *your* fault!"

Noah's mouth hangs agape as he taps his chest. "*My* fault?"

"Yours and that, that damn Christopher! You're everything, right? Even Cancer? Even Dementia? Even infertility?"

Can't argue with that.

When he doesn't respond, Maria shakes her head and sets off running.

"It's a pity you let me have this one," he tells Christopher, looking up through the falling snow. "You'd like her. She's a bitch." He pauses, sighs and sets off after her. "And she stole my handkerchief!"

Chapter Eleven
THE DETOUR

Curious about her body, Maria takes a swift detour, skidding at the end of the block to a standstill, then sets off in another direction. Luckily, Noah sees her footsteps imprinted on the ground like luminous breadcrumbs; he could snap his fingers again and appear at her side. Wound up as she is, Noah thinks it's probably best to approach with caution this time. A human would not just re-appear to block her path. He'd give chase. Besides, being dead and all, it isn't exactly an exhausting trek.

"Maria!"

He sees the back of her head through the blizzard and fears she will bolt through the traffic. A speeding truck can't kill a ghost, though.

She finds it easy to keep a steady pace

because she isn't yet panting or aching. Her muscles are tolerant of the extra strain, even as she dashes through several lanes with her eyes closed and emerges the other side of the road unharmed. She smiles and whoops, then barrels on and heads for the hospital. With any luck, she will arrive at the same time as her physical self and Marshal's corpse. She wants to see the chaos and the damage done, hoping to drive the reality of her actions home.

"Maria, slow down!" Noah orders.

She catches sight of him over her shoulder and picks up the pace. He'll try to stop her. It's important for her sanity and for the options she could face later that she sees herself as he does.

A train wreck.

As she nears, Maria is weaker; both legs give beneath her, slamming her face-first to the sidewalk, and as she pulls her body along, her arms sting and ache. Grazes appear. Deep, open wounds appear. They bleed. They're horrific. Maria cries out as she loses clear vision of the hospital doors. Her head pounds. Her brain drums against the inside of her skull, swollen.

Perhaps one of those cars mowed her down? Then, from the sensations she has now, maybe it backed over her?

"What's happening to me?"

When Noah arrives, he sits alongside her on the tarmac and cradles his knees to his chest, resting his chin upon them. It doesn't take a genius to figure out the closer she is to her body in Limbo, the more like her physical self Noah can make her feel.

She's wasting away. Weak as a rag doll.

Broken.

"My legs are—" Maria shakes her head. "I'm really paralysed, aren't I?"

Noah nods. "Well, you hit that post at an alarming speed. You'd have gone through the windscreen if you didn't have your belt on, slicing your face to shreds, too. Then you'd most *definitely* be dead. But the crumpled bonnet crushed your lower half. What... you weren't expecting human wounds to bleed human blood?" He shrugs. "They'll be telling you officially when you wake up."

"I'm still unconscious?"

"You're here with me, aren't you?"

Maria slumps, motionless. It hurts to move, breathe or think. The harder she tries to struggle against her state, the more it resists recovery.

"Why are you doing this to me?"

He looks at the sky when he hears an incoming helicopter. "Can't have you getting too close. You still have a lot to learn and you'll only upset yourself."

"I'm upset now!" Maria loses her fight. "Will I ever walk again?" she asks in a whisper.

Noah pulls his blue handkerchief from the pocket in her dress and mops her tears.

"No," he confirms after an abrupt pause.

He bends to lift her body, carrying her over his shoulder and away from the emergency department's sliding glass doors. She glances longingly at the looming building, imagining the rush of nurses and surgeons who will soon attempt to fix her numbness.

They'll fail and feel terrible for it; Maria will cause their pain today, too.

"Put me down," she tells Noah as her bruises and lacerations magically heal.

He drops Maria on her tiptoes, then braces her until the dizziness fades. The two of them stare at one another, unmoving, for a moment. This is Maria's boundary, her limit. It is as close to Marshal and herself as her spirit can bear.

"If I got any closer, would you kill me? Were those my real wounds?"

Noah blinks frantically to remove the dusting of snow that's settled on his eyelids.

"Are you willing to risk it?" he asks.

She says nothing and turns to walk away. The ambulance crew set off from the hospital on

route to another emergency and pass them by.
Maria watches with tear-filled eyes.
She's not the only person suffering today.
And Marshal isn't the only person dying.

Chapter Twelve
WHAT IS LOVE?

Maria and Noah stand side-by-side in Marshal's bedroom in their shared home, one they bought together to ease the costs of leaving the nest.

Similar in age and interests, Marshal thought they would get along well as roommates and neither found it awkward bringing home a date. Since receiving the keys for the property on day one, all their dates had been unsuccessful before it became an issue, anyway.

"Do you want to see him again?"

Maria nods. "I do. I love him."

"Do you?"

As she glances around at this small, warm reminder of her brother, she sees his personality in every painting, every choice of fabric, the colour of the carpet and his array of trinkets. On a shelf above them sits the stuffed bear he cuddled as a child, his favourite books including a few classics like *Dracula* by Bram Stoker and *20,000 Leagues Under the Sea* by Jules Verne, emphasising his love of adventure, mystery, and sometimes darkness.

Perhaps that's why he loved Maria even as she floored the gas pedal. Her soul is as dark as the deepest oceans and as merciless as a vampire's bloodlust.

Childishly, she argues, "I'd like to see you prove I *don't* love my brother. I bet you can't."

"You killed him this morning. Need I say more? You wanted to get rid of him."

"No," she corrects, running her hand along the sheets neatly folded atop his bed. "I was trying to help him. Marshal would have had to witness my mother die and then suffer through Cancer himself. Why wouldn't I offer him an exit strategy, especially if I had planned several myself? Seems only fair."

"Fair?"

"Yes, fair." She nods, satisfied.

"You took his life against his will, Maria. *How* is that fair? Didn't he deserve your respect and trust to make his own decisions?"

"It wasn't against his will. He was considering it, honestly."

"Are you sure?"

"Before the tears, yes. He said he couldn't blame me for offering, but he'd prefer to walk his path through to the end. How stupid!"

"And self-destructive?"

"Exactly."

"And suicide *isn't* self-destructive?" he asks, confused.

"I see what you're getting at, but it makes sense to me. Assisted suicide is common in other countries *and* legal. We'd agree and go together how, when and where we chose. Quickly. Comfortably. Happily and in the company of someone we love."

Noah groans and sits on the edge of the bed, sinking into the memory foam mattress. Maria scowls because whilst Noah isn't real, somehow the weight of his presence has a push on the actual world.

Then, she smirks.

I guess death puts constant pressure on us all.

He continues in the background of her thoughts. "Slamming your car into a lamppost met that criteria?"

"Fuck you, Noah. *You* didn't have to live our lives, did you?"

"As we've witnessed, I think I lived through something worse or died through something worse at least. And I had my family problems, Maria. Issues ongoing, haunting me even now. You're not the only person in existence with a dysfunctional family. If anyone understands you, it's me! Want my opinion?"

"No," she says, folding her arms.

"You're selfish."

"Everyone's selfish. We care about others until it's us versus them, then it's every man for himself or in my case, every woman. I'm no different from any other human being."

"You broke your survival instinct," he says bluntly. "So I think it's time we played a game to re-align it."

"I'm not here to play games, Noah, I'm here to learn a lesson."

Now bored with Maria's sarcasm, terrible attitude and disrespect, Noah grabs her wrist and, using it to pull her toward the bed, orders her to sit in silence. Maria bounces as she lands, further crinkling Marshal's sheets.

"You're here to do as you're told."

A pang of guilt—something Noah thought he'd never experience again—strikes his chest. He wouldn't have to act like a father-figure if she wasn't being a brat.

"I've been watching you for a while. We reapers have an inkling when someone's about to die. It's our job to be there to assist when it happens, but we shouldn't meddle."

"You're meddling now," she argues.

Noah snaps his fingers and a piece of grey masking tape appears across Maria's mouth, much to her surprise and discomfort. As she tries to remove it, she gets a glare of disapproval from her guide.

"I suggest you leave that where it is. You only need your ears until I advise otherwise." He continues, "As we watch, we learn. As we learn, we plan. And you guessed it. We plan the options you're likely to receive, which we amend according to your responses in Limbo. Are you following? You can nod or blink."

Maria nods and mumbles, "*Hmm, hmm.*"

"Good. Then I'll continue. As I was saying, it can be very frustrating for a reaper to see a client make so many mistakes but cannot interfere. There are rules," he pauses, "but if I learnt anything during my time with Christopher, rules are made to be broken. He broke a big one to offer me a special deal, which I refused. I sometimes question if I made the right decision—then I heard the universe call your name and I saw an opportunity. I *really* want to break the rules for you, Maria, but you're making it difficult to justify."

"*Hmm hmm,*" she agrees.

Marshal often told her she was stubborn and argumentative.

"I've set up three scenarios for you. In each of them, someone I've specially selected will visit you." Noah taps his chest repeatedly to emphasise this is *his* doing and not Christopher's, then continues. "They will attempt to teach you what I cannot."

"*Ich is wha*?" she mumbles.

"Which is humility, in the sense of knowing one's place in the cosmos. It's perfectly fitting."

Maria struggles. Noah rips the tape from her mouth, taking the fine blonde hair above her lip with it and causing Maria to squeak and curse him.

"What did you do that for? Can't you give me a break?"

"A taste of things to come," he snaps. "Ready?"

She rubs her upper lip and scowls as her face reddens. "I don't see how this is a game."

Noah sighs. "For every lesson you learn through these visitors, if you're still desperate to see Marshal's body, I'll reduce your pain when your spirit attempts to attend the hospital next time."

"You mean, to see myself lying there like a vegetable?"

"If you so please." He raises his brow. "Do

we have a deal?"
  Maria offers him a hand.
  Noah shakes it.
  "So, who's first?"

Chapter Thirteen
FIRST LIGHT

Christmas Day

Maria awakens to the scent of chemicals—bleach and something underlying that's sweet and sickly. Her body is almost flat beneath white sheets, and the bed is firm and uncomfortable. Her back aches as though she hasn't moved in several hours, like her muscles have seized.

She blinks against harsh white lights in panels above and follows the row of them to a pair of ugly cream curtains, wonky blinds and an empty wooden chair, save for her possessions screwed up and dumped in a clear plastic bag. She sees familiar red stains coating the inside and turns away, noticing she's in a private hospital room with the door to the corridor slightly ajar.

There's buzzing to her left, and as she strains her neck, she sees a variety of machines and monitors all checking something different like her heart rate, oxygen levels, and hanging on a metal rod out of reach is a bag of fluids.

Maria lifts her hand to her aching head, feeling the tug of tubes and cables in various places along her arms and chest; one from the bag and a few others to the machines, and as she sees dark bruising, tightly-wound bandages and carefully stitched wounds reflected in their shiny surfaces, dotted across her skin like smudged or botched tattoos, Maria gasps and hears her heartbeat increase.

"Merry Christmas," says a quiet, female voice. "Try not to move."

Maria snaps her head too quickly to find the source and pulls her neck, groaning in agony. In the chair beside her which moments ago was empty, a short, stout woman now sits. Her possessions are tucked beneath the chair and in their place is blonde hair, pale blue eyes and an unnerving smile.

"How are you?"

"Not great. I almost died," Maria replies. "Do I know you?"

"You did once."

"*Did?*"

"Yes, past tense. Did I not teach you anything?"

She tuts and adjusts her dress, which is an ankle-length polka dot sack, the same style her favourite school teacher Mrs Franks used to wear—an ex-high school teacher who offered a variety of subjects, including Maria's greatest passion, English literature. They shared a love of books. But from this teacher, she also learned kindness and friendship. After Mrs Franks arranged a meeting between her parents and the guardian of her bully, it wasn't long until that bully became her best friend and her fears of playground breaks eased.

Predominantly, though, books were a joy Mrs Franks always stimulated. Maria has always been grateful for the extra copies of fiction as a child by Enid Blyton and Roald Dahl, smuggled to her after school or during lunch breaks to read in her spare time, then return (in the same condition!). Marshal sometimes borrowed them, too, if she finished sooner than expected. Discussing each story over dinner brought the siblings closer together and encouraged their parents to include Marshal, the underachiever, in their praise.

"Recognise me now?" asks Mrs Franks, replacing a pair of silver glasses from a brown cord around her neck to the tip of her nose with a smile. "Because I remember you. You were my star pupil. I understand you went to university, too?"

"Yeah, to study literature, though I didn't use it. Have you read any memorable books lately?" Maria asks, straining and wincing through a sharp pain in her ribs. "I have Pride and Prejudice on my nightstand."

"And I on my bookshelf," Mrs Franks replies. "But literature is not why I'm here, in private, outside visiting hours."

"What did you do to bribe the nurse?"

"Nothing. I'm dead. I assumed he had briefed you."

"He? Oh, you mean Noah," Maria says, her smile weakening. "You're my first visitor, right?"

"Unfortunately for me."

Maria is offended. "*Unfortunately?*"

"What, you think I haven't got better things to do than re-teach you the basics of being human? My husband and I are finally together again and I was so happy when that delightful man, Christopher, extinguished my light. George and I don't have eternity to be together —I was trying to make the most of his company."

"Weren't you permanently reunited?"

Mrs Franks narrows her eyes. "Because of

you! It was the option I chose. George and I were to remain together until *you* behaved like the 11-year-old you once were, which Christopher said you might never do. And yet, here we are. Seems your actions were predictable."

"I'm sorry, I don't quite follow."

Mrs Franks adjusts her dress and grumbles. "Drive cars into posts in your own time, dear, not mine. I've earned a peaceful afterlife, and it's the afterlife I could have chosen. Instead, I'm resolving more childish antics!"

"No offence, but didn't *you* chose this path? Why didn't you opt to be with George forever instead of here fixing my mess?"

"*When* will you grow up?"

"I have grown up!"

Maria struggles to sit, using only her weakened wrists as leverage. Her legs, as she already expected, are useless and limp, wrapped in white cloth. Mrs Franks reaches out to lift Maria's pillow for support, but she shakes her head and bats away her fingers.

"I don't need your help. I can manage on my own."

"Beyond help, are we? The Queen of the Universe—that's how you're behaving, like a selfish, privileged brat. Your actions affect the lives of others. People die for each other every day. I died for someone. You'll die for someone. And that Noah, he died for someone too; a person he now cares for tremendously."

"Noah isn't human. He doesn't care for anything. He can't."

"In a rather unique way, he can. *Does*. Your feelings and what *you* want isn't what the Earth revolves around."

Scolded, Maria's bottom lip quivers. "I'm sorry, I didn't—"

"I'll just unplug all these beeping things and tell the nurses to go home early. What's the point in them wasting their time with you, Princess Maria, when they can save the patients who haven't thrown their entire existence in the faces of their loved ones?"

Maria scoffs. "You were so nice to me in school!"

"If you remember, we also had words occasionally. I was your teacher then so I'm your teacher, not your friend nor your mother— your biological one, anyway."

"I never knew my biological mother so you may very well be."

Mrs Franks scowls. "I'm here to make it clear you're *not* the deity you think you are."

"You can't turn anything off anyway, you're dead." Maria folds her arms.

Mrs Franks shrugs. "Be smart with me if you like, but it won't change the fact you'll be spending the rest of your life in a wheelchair. Nobody is beyond help, Maria. Noah granted me *some* power, just in case—to help you. To accept help is the natural, expected thing to do, and it doesn't make you weak. It shouldn't be embarrassing."

"I'm neither of those things. I just want to do this on my own. I must at some point. May as well start as I mean to go on."

Shaking her head, Mrs Franks continues, "I'm disappointed in you. Such a confident, bright and well-educated woman ought to know better. Suicide? Murder? There are cops on their way. Noah said I'd have to hurry this lesson along a bit as not to overstay my welcome or terrify those hard-working humans."

"Yes, yes, my accident is inconvenient for everyone, I get it."

"What happened to you wasn't an accident."

"What did he tell you about my 'accident' anyway?" Maria says, scowling as she demonstrates the lie with air quotes.

"Enough. Your brother was dying and you wanted to spare him the pain. Your mother struggles with her memory and you cannot carry a child of your own. All perfectly valid reasons to be sad—depressed, even. Suicidal?

No. Homicidal? Nonsense. Yet, you ignored *everyone's* wishes and made this all about you."

"My brother agreed with me!"

Mrs Franks stands abruptly. "*That's* a lie. You told Noah Marshal had asked to walk his own path, be it the Cancer or otherwise that ended him."

"He considered it, at least."

"You still acted against his wishes. Selfish. Single-minded. *Shame* on you!"

Maria imagines throwing her pillow at the old crow. She knew what was best for her brother and he would never have blamed her for trying to help him. In fact, Queen of the Universe sounded like a job she'd be fabulous at. Sometimes, she knew what was best for people before they admitted they even needed something to begin with. Sure, the end of this last example didn't quite play out as she'd planned. But, it was a damn sight better than letting him waste away.

"How about you just tell me why you're here, Mrs Franks, then both of us can get back to what we're supposed to be doing? You dying and moving on to your less-than-you-expected afterlife. Me, well, dying probably too. Burning in Hell." She sneers and folds her arms. "Oh, wait a second...IT DOESN'T EXIST!"

"That's the most sense I've had out of you so

far today." Mrs Franks sits back down beside her. "I'm here to teach you a lesson. You need to understand your place in the universe. You're a microbe in an ocean of wonder, young lady. Have some humility!"

"I do!"

With a grimace, she says, "You *do not* have a modest opinions of your self-importance."

Maria deflates, shuffling uncomfortably as Mrs Franks basks in her knowledge and the glory of putting her ex-pupil in her place at the bottom of the spiritual food chain.

"You're *here*," she says, showing on an imaginative vertical ruler that Maria is at the bottom. She's ant shit, lowest of the low. "And Noah is here," she continues, shooting her palm way up to (but not quite touching) the top. "Then there's Christopher and his cosmos, his universe and the unwritten rules we play by." Now she reaches the breaking point. "*Long* way to go."

"Unwritten rules? How are we expected to know what they are, then?"

"Oh, stop making excuses."

She smacks the back of Maria's hands with the imaginative ruler, using a brutal amount of force; pain may be the only way to get this smarmy, bull-headed urchin to listen to her. And Maria actually feels the sting of its contact.

She shakes her hands. *"Bitch!"*

"That I am, but *I* wear my label proudly. Darkness and denial have captured you, convinced you what you did was a generous thing... justified. That it was your God-given right to mess with the universe's plans. I'm sorry, but it's about time you opened your eyes to let the first slither of light in."

"Light? A metaphor for what, exactly?"

Mrs Franks snaps the imaginary ruler over her knee. As she throws it to the ground, Maria sees it materialise and clatter against the half-open door. It draws the attention of a passing nurse.

"My job!" she says.

When Maria turns to the chair, Mrs Franks is no longer there.

Chapter Fourteen
DOCTOR'S ORDERS

The nurse calls for a doctor to check on Maria. She hears voices and a clatter coming from the room and shows him the broken ruler in the doorway—snapped in two as if trapped in a hinge.

Maria slides in and out of consciousness. She's smiling because she knows what really happened.

It's the expression she holds when Noah Finn steps up to join her in the corridor of her old primary school.

The halls are smaller. Maria is much older and taller than she was the last time she walked to class and as they peer through into a locker room, she sees a square pigeon hole and peg with her name above it and the pink coat she loved so much hanging neatly.

Maria's eyes fill with tears. "I liked this school. It was fun."

"Elementary school is, because there's no responsibility and life is relatively easy."

"Hmm," she says in agreement, but nothing further.

Her eyes glaze as they walk further down the hall, passing excited children skipping in the opposite direction, heading for lunch. Instead of shuddering or complaining about how weird the sensation is of having ghostly children pass through her frame, or questioning why those children can't see them, Maria accepts this is a vision of her past and she's about to run into the woman who just chastised her.

"It's good to be back here," she says. "If you've been watching me my entire life, Noah, you'll know I almost stayed to teach the next generation English literature in a local school like she did."

"But you didn't."

"No, I didn't."

"Christopher witnessed your struggle and your failure."

"Failure is such a harsh word," she says.

"Harsh but the truth. You did well at university, top of your class, but you've always known to work in a school would have been a mistake."

"I'm not so sure. I often regret not accepting the job offer."

"Your body knew before your soul that it could not bear a child. Psychologically, seeing children every day would have been too much so choosing not to accept that job, Maria, was a defence mechanism."

Noah wrings his hands together before Maria can answer or argue against his theory, then shoves the door to their left. It opens into a large classroom, lined with bookshelves and drawers, trays and pots of pens and pencils. There are paintings, laminated pages about the alphabet and basic mathematics, dinosaur names even Noah can't pronounce, and an outline of the human body decorating the walls. Dangling from the ceiling are cut-outs of the solar system and stars, all labelled accurately and as neatly as the children can manage at that age.

Maria's eyes skip all of this and find the square of speckled carpet in the far corner where a teacher sits on a plastic chair, surrounded by cross-legged kids listening intently as she reads aloud. They're younger than Maria was when she met Mrs Franks for the first time, but they seem to love her just as strongly.

She leads Noah to the table where she once sat. The chair is tiny and the tables are lower than she remembers, but she grins all the same and wonders if she'll still fit without breaking something.

She daydreams about drinking her milk in the morning and singing in an assembly around 10 o'clock in the gym where, two hours later, she would eat her lunch. Though her family weren't religious and never attended church on a Sunday, she still sang along to every hymn and practised the values the school promoted.

Noah sighs and places a hand on her shoulder. "Are you alright?"

She shrugs his hand away.

"Story time," Maria mouths, "was on Tuesdays, intended to inspire us and spike our creativity for the afternoon. My favourite lesson, if you can call it one."

"Children love stories."

"Because we can live elsewhere for a while," Maria explains, "and escape the pressures of the world. Oh, I know you doubt children suffer much at that age, but I did. I was ill a lot and missed mathematics and science, physical education and art. I had terrible allergies and thankfully, they eased as I aged, but I always made the extra effort, no matter how serious the doctor said they were, to be present for story time." She pauses, saddened. "I think that's why my parents paid less attention to Marshal than they did to me—I needed them more."

"Marshal's world continued regardless," Noah agrees, "but we all get knocked off our axis sometimes. We will never stop needing our parents, even when they leave this world."

"He was a lot more prone to accidents than me, though," she says, laughing. "He broke his leg falling out of a tree, pretending to be Indiana Jones or something. Twisted his ankle falling down the stairs, too, excited for the delivery of a new bike which he couldn't ride for weeks after. Snapped off his front tooth about a month after, jumping a makeshift ramp in the street and landing on his chin. Bike was OK, though."

She sniffles. Marshal sometimes let her select a colourful character-splattered bandage for his cuts and grazes when he landed awkwardly after another of his garden-based adventures. She also chose his cast colours at the hospital... every time.

"Wait, you don't think he injured himself on purpose, do you, for attention?"

Noah shrugs and listens as she tells other anecdotes, smiling through some and crying through others.

She doesn't need the answer.
She already knows.

But, she promises Noah she doesn't regret not spending more time at school. Being sick meant spending extra days with her family, learning how to run a household: cooking and cleaning, doing laundry, fixing electronics. They'd all prepare her to become a mother herself, no doubt caring for a sick child should they inherit her poor luck. As she saw her mother in action, it made Maria want to start a family. She was excited to step into her mother's shoes and was always told she'd make a tentative parent.

But, it was not to be.

Chapter Fifteen
FRANK'S SENSE

Maria rubs her aching head from another sudden transition between the classroom and her car. Occasionally, her vision blurs or twists, causing her to topple sideways until she regains her balance. With Noah's help, she fastens her seatbelt and grips the steering wheel, hoping it will ground her.

It's snowing heavily now. The car is freezing. Noah leans across to start the ignition.

"You failed your first lesson," he tells her, shaking his head. "I'm a little disappointed but not surprised."

"What was the first lesson supposed to be? I think I learnt a lot from Mrs Franks."

"In the past you did, but today you're still stubborn and arrogant. I expected this might happen. Poor Mrs Franks agreed to help you and she gave up—"

"Time with her dead husband. I've already been on that guilt trip."

"And arrived back safely, I see. Why didn't you learn not to be selfish and to let other people be?"

"Be what?"

"Just *be*!" Noah growls. "Be in charge of their own lives. Be right occasionally. Be able to make mistakes. Belong to their thoughts, emotions, wants and needs." He shakes his fists. "*Why* can you not see how it's equally effective to help with words and not actions sometimes? Only a selfish person would kill their brother to satisfy a need for peace and harmony—a need to be in charge of everything. Only a selfish person would then commit suicide and leave her other relatives—one of whom is sick—to suffer such a tragedy because she couldn't have her way."

"I didn't steal Mrs Franks's afterlife on purpose. I'm not *that* selfish. I'm rather offended you'd think it."

Maria lowers her head. Perhaps she hadn't dealt so well with her family's troubles. Nor had she considered how her mother would feel or how it might progress her illness, following the death of both her children at the same time.

Too late now.

Frustrated, Maria's hands tighten around the wheel, forcing the blood from her knuckles to her fingertips.

"Something even children understand, Maria, is it's not up to *us* to decide the fate of others because of our high opinion of ourselves. Sometimes, you need to understand another person's ideas and systems might be better."

"Fine, so that sounds like me," she mumbles and picks at her fingernails.

"We are as others see us, Maria, and Marshal looked up to you. Your parents relied on you and they danced around your mental health issues because of your illnesses, placing you on a pedestal you shouldn't have been on. You were not sane when you hit that accelerator and you weren't capable of assessing the situation; your clouded judgment that it was your responsibility to control the outcome of every tragedy and the emotional responses everyone —in your mind—should have had, only stirred a destructive potion which led you to the Hudson."

"My parents and my brother and everyone else in my life caused me to become some impatient psychopath?" She shook her head. "That can't be true."

"They weren't the cause but they were also not the solution."

"It makes sense, I suppose," she agrees.

Noah squeezes her hand. He waits a moment, allowing her epiphany to sink in.

"Are you OK?"

Maria exhales deeply as a weight lifts from her shoulders. Though they are not light enough yet, Noah predicts with the help of her teacher's latest lesson on how to be a decent human being, he'll finally get through to her.

It's not enough, Mrs Franks, but it's a start!

Chapter Sixteen
A DELIVERY

Maria gasps for air as she sits, bolt upright, in her hospital bed. Alarms on the machines sound and she's sweating profusely, mortified by her latest nightmare—an encounter with Noah and her old English teacher, Mrs Franks.

She failed that teacher immensely when she threw everything school had taught her away. She'd forgotten her rightful place in her family unit, in her community, in the *world*. They were right; she had no right to make her brother's last decision for him.

"Miss Shephard," prompts a husky male voice to her left. "My name is Doctor Motley and I've been overseeing your care. Can you hear me?"

Dr Motley prompts two nurses to hurry to her aid, fixing her up with fresh bandages, changing dressings and wiping her forehead. One nurse pours her a glass of cool water while the other checks wires and the drip to ensure nothing came loose during her thrashing.

"Do you know what date it is?"

"Christmas Eve," she mumbles.

Dr Motley corrects her, but she doesn't seem at all phased she's in a hospital bed on Christmas Day.

"I had a nightmare."

She takes a sip of water through a straw, then repeats herself.

"You're safe now. Do you remember what happened to you?"

"I was in an accident," she says, blinking rapidly through sweat stinging her eyes. A nurse wipes her brow. "We hit a tree."

"Close enough," he advises, making notes. "Has anyone explained your injuries yet?"

Maria shakes her head. "I can guess."

"Miss Shephard—"

She dismisses any medical explanations.

"There was damage to my spine. I'm paralysed from the waist down. I kind of figured when I woke up and couldn't feel my legs. But I'm hoping soon I will, even if it's all in my head."

"That's called Phantom Limb Syndrome," he tells her, scribbling as the nurses shout abbreviated reports after examining her body for the 100th time. "Usually when somebody has an amputation."

"When can I go home?"

"Not yet, I'm afraid. It's Christmas Day; we can't get most of your tests done until the 27th. Can I call someone for you?"

"Just my dad, but tell him not to come down here. My mum needs him at home."

As a consolation, Dr Motley informs her there's an enormous bunch of flowers at the nurse's station with her name on from someone called Noah.

"Noah?"

"Is he your husband?"

"No," she says, sinking into the sheets as far as her body and the pain will allow. "Can I see them?"

"I'll have a nurse bring them in, though we're not supposed to." Dr Motley pauses, sighs and puts a gentle hand on her shoulder. "It could be much worse. You're really very lucky."

"And my brother?"

Dr Motley removes his hand. "I'm sorry to tell you that he didn't make it."

"I assumed as much," she says, turning away. On second thought, she turns back and gestures at the door. "When the cops arrive, you can show them straight in."

"If you're sleeping, I will advise—"

"Wake me," she says, abruptly. "It's about time I considered others. I'll rest when I've confessed."

Chapter Seventeen
A RIVER OF TEARS

Maria cries herself to sleep when the doctor and his entourage of busy nurses leave the room. She is blessed with solitude and darkness, drifting into an abyss of nothingness—the punishment Maria now agrees she deserves.

In the distance, there is a light. Gentle at first then bright and guiding.

She has learnt her lesson.

She reaches out to grab it, hoping to see Noah again so she can prove how sorry she is for the hasty decisions she's made. He and Mrs Franks were right about her brother's last moments.

Your death, your decision, she tells herself.

The light illuminates, suddenly blinding her, and out steps Noah, prompting a fresh scene to unfold.

Noah Finn & the Art of Conception

She's in a wide courtyard fenced in by wire, supported every few hundred metres by a tall brick tower. There are men with guns pointing down where Maria sits in a wheelchair. Her fingers find the rubber of the tyres beneath and, when she reaches over, they graze gravel. Maria wheels forward a couple of inches, listening to the comforting crunch of her wheels against the stones, and she closes her eyes.

"Is this my future?" she asks Noah.

He snaps his fingers.

Before her appears a brown wooden bench, the kind you see in a park or a school yard. He sits, his elbows resting on his knees. He doesn't reply, though.

"I get it," she says, "and I understand. The punishment should fit the crime, right?"

"Right," he responds.

Behind her, several other women in pyjama-style overalls pass by; she hears their harsh language and catches sight of some intricate tattoos—colourful sleeves on at least half the women and skulls or curse words on the others. They are strong and intimidating and Maria suddenly feels the swelling of her right eye and the tenderness in her ribs where they have beaten her.

"They don't like me much, do they?"

"I can reveal the rest of your injuries since

arriving here if you like?"

"I get the point. I fill my future with pain, self-loathing and torture."

"Only if you fail this next test," he says and hops off the bench, disappearing in her peripheral vision.

Maria is alone for the next few minutes, observing the courtyard and what life in prison might be like on Christmas Day. Some women are smiling and talking about their families. One or two have phoned their children and others have visitors later.

Maria already knows she will spend the day alone.

A few of the guards eye her suspiciously, as though they assume at any point she might spring up out of her chair and yell *surprise!* before stabbing someone. They don't want to be working on Christmas Day; guarding a bunch of monsters is not their ideal holiday.

Maria turns away, wheeling across the courtyard at a steady pace. It isn't long before her arms tire and a woman approaches, ignoring the others who are staring at them.

"Not as easy as it looks?"

She is older than most of the inmates. Her hair is grey and her skin shows lines around her mouth and eyes. Perhaps in her early 60's.

Either that or she frowns a lot, which in an establishment like this one is believable.

"Who are you?"

"My name is Liz. My son is Emmanuel Mirh," she says, leading Maria to a set of stone steps where she sits, mimicking Noah's earlier posture. "He lived near to you. He was in the accident that killed your brother."

Maria realises now this must be the mother of the guy in a coma—the driver of the pickup truck who hit her from behind, crushing them against the post. She wants to apologise for causing her son's state, to tell her she wishes he'd wake up so she could apologise in person and explain everything.

Despite her age, Liz looks terrifying. Prison has hardened her to the cruelty of other people. Her crime is unknown—something serious—so Maria doubts she's here for a pathetic excuse.

It could never be enough.

"Is this real?" Maria asks her.

Liz shakes her head. "No, it's part of my past and your future. Noah has, for your next lesson, merged the two to give us a few moments together before I move on."

"I see," Maria says, lowering her gaze.

Liz laughs. "Oh, don't beat around the bush, I'm aware I'm dead and even more deserving than you of my fate. I'm still pissed at you for harming my son, but compared to his mother, you're an angel. I've served my time though... almost."

"What did you do?"

She shakes her head and shuffles, trying to find a comfortable spot on the stone stairs. Maria notices there is no ramp to allow for her easy access to the building—should this version of the future be her path, she will have to rely on the kindness of others to carry her inside. It lingers in the back of her mind. She will be at the mercy of the women sharing her block.

She will be at the mercy of villains.

But she, too, is a villain.

"Are you going to tell me what happened to Emmanuel?" asks Liz.

"Seems everyone knows everything before me."

"Remind me."

"You're asking because admitting my error is part of this next lesson, I assume." Maria sighs. "It won't mean much now, but I'm very sorry I involved your son. Really. I didn't mean for anyone else to get hurt. This was between my brother and I; not concentrating and driving way too fast, hell-bent on it being our last day on Earth together. I swerved and Emmanuel, well, he panicked and couldn't stop in time."

"He was behind you?"

"Wrong place, wrong time," Maria says. "I'm not proud of my actions and I'm seeing how foolish and selfish I was to attempt suicide and, I guess, homicide. The outcome cannot be changed, but I can aid your understanding of my intentions and I assure you, Emmanuel shouldn't have been there. He's in a coma, so I hear."

"Hear from who?"

"Noah. He says he's Death, but I think he's more like a guardian angel than a reaper, working for someone who is *definitely* Death. Are you my second visitor, my second ghost?"

"I guess so."

She rolls up her sleeves to reveal defined muscles and, like the other women, faded tattoos. It's obvious there's a gym here, and she's learned how to protect herself, something Maria will probably have to try even from her wheelchair. She wonders if it's possible to use it as a weapon, or at least to conceal something for self-defence purposes.

"We're stuck here until you learn the next lesson," she confirms.

"Which is what?"

"Incarceration."

Liz folds her fingers outward, stretching her

wrists, arms and clicking her fingers all at once. She seems strong physically and emotionally. Maria envies her knowledge of life behind these fences and, if they had more time, would ask her how to survive.

"I can define incarceration for you," Maria replies confidently. "It means to put someone or something in prison or an enclosure."

"Not so much a definition as a reality check to prepare you for your options. I never liked zoos, though," Liz tells her, picking dirt from the bottom of her dusty black pumps. "Much prefer to study animals in their natural habitats. In here, it's not the same thing, but there are easy comparisons." She pauses for a moment to crack her neck, making her seem even more deadly. "When survival or leadership is at stake, human beings turn to violence and savagery. May the best woman win. Sleep with one eye open. All those crappy clichés, that only make sense when you're facing their advice, now mean something."

"Is that how you survived in here? You resorted to brutality?"

"I'm not proud, but I lived longer than I expected."

"Didn't you make any friends?"

"Alliances. Gangs. No friends."

"Why not?" Maria asks. "Surely you met

someone who shared your ideals, your fears? You didn't trust anyone, not even a guard?"

"I *especially* avoided them. They may favour you one day, but the next they'll favour your enemies. No use relying on their protection. You can't trust anyone in here, sometimes not even yourself."

"But why? These women are human beings just like you and me."

"I was afraid of death, of anyone stronger or more capable than me; of being *literally* stabbed in the back. Turns out, that's how I died."

"They stabbed you?" Maria's mouth hangs agape. She scans the yard, searching for the killer. "How? When?"

"In line at the cafeteria with a sharpened plastic spoon. Here," she says, patting where her kidney would be.

"For what reason?"

"They didn't need one," Liz says, shrugging. She keeps her head low; even in death, she dare not meet the gaze of the inmates. "Must have offended or threatened someone, somehow."

"I'm sorry," Maria says. And she is, genuinely. "But I don't envy you being so deeply incarcerated."

Liz scowls. "What do you mean?"

"You shut down—turned off your interest and emotions. You led a lonely existence, even behind these walls. This should have been your opportunity for rehabilitation. Didn't you study or read books or the Bible, at least?" Maria asks, shocked by how little this woman did with so much time on her hands. "I'm not religious, but I've read it."

"Good for you, but that's not what—"

"I'd have taken some courses or volunteered to work in the library or something."

"You know nothing of prison life," Liz says, laughing. "I did as you said at first, but then my focus shifted to protection."

"And it did you no good."

"We all die, Maria. Some before our time. No matter what. No matter where, when or how. Our deaths mean life for another."

"I disagree."

"Then you're stupid."

"Maybe," she says, gesturing at her wheelchair and their surroundings. "Takes a fool to recognise a fool, it seems. But you need not be here *now*," Maria tells her, honestly. "I know the meaning of incarceration; it's what I've been doing to myself since I learned I couldn't have children. You should have chosen a happier afterlife."

"You locked your truth and identity away?" Emmanuel's mother asks, ignoring Maria's suggestion that this crappy afterlife is self-inflicted.

"I never really socialised enough to explore it. All my female friends were getting married and having children and I'd taken a step in the opposite direction," she explained, "so their company no longer appealed to me. I was jealous and, to be honest, just wanted to scream at them, *'how can you not see my pain?'* Emotionally and mentally, I hid from my trauma and imprisoned myself. I tried to hide my feelings and improve my lifestyle with medication, yoga and goodness knows how many self-help books, but in doing so I drove myself to commit an act of murder and attempted suicide. I hurt your son, and I totalled my car."

Liz sighs and stands, straining as she does so. Maria can see a red stain where her wound once existed.

"If you're asking for my forgiveness, there's no point," she says, now scowling at Maria as if staring through her. "I can't give you that."

Maria's gaze doesn't falter this time. She looks Liz right in the eye.

"I'm not asking. But I *am* sorry."

"Yes, you are. And it seems you're still incarcerated even though, in reality, you're not here yet."

Maria nods. "In the hospital. In the

wheelchair. I've thought about it *in depth*."

Liz laughs; it's a throaty laugh—a little distant, telling Maria their time together is possibly ending.

"I bet you have."

"So what's the lesson? Have I passed?"

Liz wrings her hands together and takes a step closer to Maria. Now she looms above her and Maria can truly appreciate her height and build. She's a giant.

"It's not so much a lesson as a favour."

"I owe you that at least."

Liz grunts. "It's both a favour and a way for us to move on. We each get what we wanted. You learn that sometimes imprisoning yourself the way you have is more punishment than you deserve. We all go to the same place."

Maria remembers Noah telling her there is no such thing as Heaven, Hell, sin or any of the labels humans apply to places or items in their lifetime. There is only the universe.

"What's the favour?" When Liz hesitates, she frowns. "Go on, ask away."

"It's not something you can say, it's something you can *do*."

"You want me to visit Emmanuel when I wake up? I was going to do that anyway."

"No," she says sheepishly. "Though I appreciate the sentiment."

"Then what? Come on. The sooner you tell me, the sooner you get to move on."

Suddenly, Liz's hands are around Maria's throat and are squeezing; her lungs are burning and she's panicking, flailing her arms in Liz's face to poke her in the eye or distract her long enough to escape. The colour drains from her cheeks and her energy levels drop as she chokes to death.

Maria's vision becomes a mass of cloud but nothing more. Emmanuel's mother is as burly as she looks! There's a ringing in her ears and, suddenly, a stillness in her chest.

Everything goes black.

"*Die*," Liz whispers as she disappears up the stone steps.

Maria wonders if she's about to comply.

Chapter Eighteen
WHEN ALL IS LOST

There's ticking in the room with her, somewhere, and it won't shut up. Maria imagines a clock counting down to her third and final visitor. It's louder than her watch, but the tick-tock is all she can hear; it's consuming her senses because, as she regains consciousness, Maria cannot yet see anything in the hospital room so is relying on her ears for a change.

"It's alright, Maria," Noah says, taking her hand. His skin brushes hers like pins and needles. "You've learned a precious lesson. It may take a while for you to come round completely. She strained your soul."

"She tried to kill me," Maria croaks, feeling the lingering ache in her windpipe and her delicate skin. "I apologised, and she still tried to kill me."

"Because that was the closure she needed. Death is your lesson. That it is naturally inevitable and so we need not interfere. She needed to kill the woman who hurt her son; violence is how she has always led her life, and violence is how it ended. But she'll have time to redeem herself because she chose her afterlife wisely."

"They murdered her in prison," Maria tells him.

"She deserved her imprisonment in life, Maria. The judge sentenced her fairly. But her story and her options matter not at the moment. What matters is yours; did you learn anything?"

"More than I expected I would. I'm incarcerated even now; I can barely see or smell you, but I hear you loud and clear. Perhaps that's what I've been lacking all along, the ability and mental capacity to hear what people have been telling me and to accept their help and advice. I saw them pity me as they hugged me, but I didn't listen to what they were *telling* me."

"Which was what?" Noah prompts, gifting her with her sense of smell as a reward.

Maria inhales and smiles. The nurses must have delivered the flowers. Noah left roses; she knows they're fresh and vibrant despite being unable to see them yet.

"They love me. The countless offers to attend therapy with me or at least to drive me to and from appointments. The doctor's advice for my prescription drugs which I often refused to take, the shared stories of the other women at the discussion group and the videos on-line I watched, but paid little attention to." Maria pauses and flaps her hands, fighting back tears. "The only voice I heard was when the doctor gave us the grave news and when my boyfriend, Joey, said he could no longer be with me. After that, I drowned out the entire world."

Noah squeezes her hand a little tighter until Maria smiles at the warmth of his comforting touch. He returns her sight, watching tears flow freely down her cheeks. She is not alone, and right now his guidance means everything.

"You've done well so far, Maria," he tells her. "Mrs Mirh volunteered her services for another favour—she agreed to help you break free of your self-inflicted incarceration. You were both overly punishing yourselves. Now, she can move on. Hopefully, so can you."

"I think I understand. She's been watching over Emmanuel, angry with herself for being unable to protect him when in prison and then from her afterlife. But, he's been surviving well enough without her and, I am sure, she's pleased he's turned out better than she did.

Then some lunatic woman in a little green car swerves in front of him and brakes without warning, sending him lurching forward in his seat and landing him in a coma." Maria blinks rapidly, pleased to be regaining her eyesight. "I'd want to throttle me, too."

Noah chuckles. "You didn't earn her forgiveness."

"No," Maria says, "but that's OK because I don't deserve it and, in all fairness, I didn't ask. I'm assuming my task wasn't to earn it, anyway?"

"It wasn't, but don't you want her to forgive you for hurting an innocent man?"

"Nobody is innocent," she corrects, "and hearing her say she forgives me would have been wonderful, but I'd like his first—he's the one I hurt. I need to earn forgiveness and a five-minute visit in a prison yard isn't sufficient time for me to do that. I'm sure it will not be the last I see of her."

"How so?"

"If I don't die this time around, I'll die eventually and we'll meet in the afterlife. Gives me time to gather my evidence."

"What evidence might that be?" Noah asks.

Maria shrugs. "Oh, a list of all my good deeds to show her I've been a better person since. A history of my behaviour. Then she can decide. Is my heart lighter than a feather?"

"That's not really what happens." He tuts. "She's given you a precious gift, Maria, just as Mrs Franks did."

Scrunching her face, she says, "I see that *now*. I'm sure my heart is not lighter than a feather, nor would most people's be. I've sinned before and I'll sin again."

"Here's an important reminder," Noah says, curling his finger until she leans in to hear a whisper. "There are no such things as sins. And it's a relief, right? There's no good or bad, no light or dark, innocent or evil. Not really, anyway. Still worth being a likeable person who doesn't murder their brother or attempt to kill themselves. But, at the base of everything, there is just life. And life is all we have; don't segregate or compartmentalise. You cannot label it. Christopher taught me things just are. Life just is. We're just here. There's nothing else to it. How does *that* make you feel?"

Maria nibbles her bottom lip. "In all honesty?"

"In all honesty," he repeats, wondering what else she'd tell him if he allowed her to lie.

"Kind of lost," she says, "and lonely."

"Lonely?"

"All these years I've hoped there was a meaning and a point to everything, though I haven't fully believed in a God."

"You read the Bible."

"Yes, I've believed in fate and Hell and assumed I'd end up there. But now I know the human mind creates these things."

"Technically, we base them on *some* fact. The universe has a plan, but it's not set in stone. Things change and free will interferes, but the course corrects itself. Christopher deals with everyone's afterlife, but instead of punishing someone, he gives them suitable options for the good of the universe, not just the good of the individual. Some options are more impressive than others if that person has lived an amazing life because the option they choose will continue to pay that forward. Murderers and thieves, not so much, but their options are never punishments because we have to learn lessons before *anyone* can move on. It's the way he runs things."

"It's a suitable business model," she agrees, nodding. "Still a little deflating. Do you remember how you reacted when Christopher told you there was no God, no religion, nothing?"

"Disappointed too for a while. Until I realised he wasn't telling me there's *nothing* out there, he was telling me that there's *everything*, but humans aren't capable of seeing or understanding it. Our minds can't comprehend the sheer brilliance of the universe. It's too impressive so we break it down into chunks of things we can comprehend. Like a maths puzzle." He grins, mashing his hands together as if to squish or crumple something between them. "I always hated maths, but still, you get my point?"

"I get your point," Maria says, smiling. "Thank you."

"For what?"

"Telling me the truth and opening my eyes."

"So, what was the second lesson?"

Maria's eyes brighten. "Ye of little faith! Incarceration."

"*I* could have told you that! What have you learned, Maria? Details! Details! If you want to see your brother pain-free..."

"Oh," she says, blushing. She pauses, then confidently replies, "That we're all in unnecessary prisons, even if self-inflicted and imaginary. That pain doesn't exist; we create it and suffer internally when it just doesn't matter. I don't think I want or need to see Marshal now, Noah."

"Why not?"

"Because," she says, "my actions were, I mean *are*, all pointless—I was never in pain to begin with."

Chapter Nineteen
ANY SUGGESTIONS?

Maria's functioning limbs ache and tense as the painkillers in her system fade. She's due another dose, and like an addict, she cannot wait for the nurse to arrive with her needle. Not only that, but since her last discussion with Noah, Maria has realised her clothing needs changing.

She hasn't showered or used the toilet since she woke. Now she's paralysed. Someone will have to assist. It's gross and embarrassing, so she hopes it happens soon.

I guess with a loss of your legs comes a loss of your dignity.

"Maria?"

Maria jumps from her depression when the doctor sticks his head around the door, still clutching her notes and his stethoscope.

"Are you my third visitor?"

He's puzzled, so says nothing. She waves him in and smiles as convincingly as she can, now resigned to the fact she will never walk again, will never use the bathroom the same, and will never enjoy a man's company.

A man like the doctor.

She hadn't noticed before but he's handsome, around 5'9" with brown hair and hazel eyes.

"*Please* tell me you're not here to bathe me?"

The doctor's eyes widen. "No," he says, then laughs. "A nurse will be along later to help you with that. I'm just here on my rounds."

He asks some questions about her pain levels, what she remembers about the accident and how she feels emotionally and mentally.

Would she like to see a psychotherapist? Does she need to talk to friends or family?

Maria shows willing to get the doctor off her back, then asks for an estimated arrival time of the Police. He tells her they're on their way.

"Would you like some paper and a pen to make notes for when they arrive? Sometimes it helps if you jot memories down. I find I can better piece together timelines and things I need to remember—important facts, figures."

Maria thanks him and, as he turns to leave, she asks, "Any suggestions?"

"Pardon?"

"Do you have any suggestions for me?"

"Concerning..."

"My circumstances. My condition. My future. How am I supposed to cope with being stuck in a wheelchair for the rest of my life? How am I supposed to accept what I can no longer do?"

"Well," he says, his face solemn and his tone serious, "if I were you, I'd be thankful there are still things you're capable of."

"What do you mean?"

He gestures at a photograph of her brother, Marshal, in a frame beside her bed; a photograph she didn't know she owned or was even in the room.

Another gift from Noah, no doubt.

"It could be worse," he says and closes the door behind him.

Chapter Twenty
THE INTERVIEW

When two Policemen arrive, Maria is wide awake and ready for them. She wonders if they represent her third visitor. She's written the series of events as she remembers them and at the moment it's her word against, well, against nobody else's. The other guy is in a coma, and her brother is dead. Everyone directly involved is in the room and witnesses can only speculate externally.

Maria swallows hard to answer their first question.

"How are you?" the first officer asks.

She nicknames him Officer Curly because of his fluffy black hair like a sheep's wool and the smile lines around his mouth. He has kind brown eyes and is slimmer than his partner, who is a stocky, 6'2" bald man wearing a scowl. He never speaks.

She wonders if this will be a case of 'good cop, bad cop'.

They needn't bother.

She has nothing to hide.

Maria answers, "Sore, but lucky to have escaped with my life. At least, *now* I feel lucky, I didn't then."

"Your intended to commit suicide?" Curly asks, jotting something in his electronic pocketbook. "I understand your brother was in the vehicle with you to change your mind."

"No, he got in under false pretences," Maria explains. "Our family's been through a lot. It has depressed me for a long time." She inhales deeply and starts from the beginning. "My mother has Dementia and my brother found out he has—had?—Cancer. My boyfriend left me when he learnt I couldn't have children. I tried to get help, but therapy served only as a constant reminder I needed it. When one path leads to a brick wall, I'm worse off."

"So you contemplated ending your life?"

"I planned to drive into the Hudson. Marshal would have had to see my mother die and then die himself after an agonizing few months. And it wasn't fair. So I told him about my plan to kill myself and why. He understood, and he said he was sorry. I needed a way out."

"He tried to stop you?"

Maria nodded. "Not through a fight or anything. We just had words. Eventually, I suggested he should come with me. My mother wouldn't know any different; soon she'd forget the entire thing anyway, and he and I could come to a controlled, peaceful ending with less suffering than we were both enduring."

"He *agreed?*" Curly asks, surprised.

"He thanked me for trying to understand and trying to help him in my hmm, how did he say it, 'fucked up backwards way'? Marshal always had a way with words." She smiles. "Anyway, he asked me to postpone suicide so we could spend the day together. I think he was trying to distract me and change my mind. I agreed, at the time."

"At the time?"

"Well, yeah. We got talking later in the car, argued, and well..."

"You hit the accelerator. He tried to stop you."

"We fought over the steering wheel and I swerved, not realising there was anyone behind me. The pickup smashed into the back of us and pushed my car into the lamppost. When I woke up, Marshal wasn't moving or breathing and he was staring at me with this haunted expression. I knew he was dead. I couldn't feel my legs.

Dunno how long I was out."

"Did *you* call for help?"

Maria shakes her head. "A witness did. And then I saw—"

"Saw?" prompts Curly, gently.

"It doesn't matter. You wouldn't believe me."

"Try me."

Maria throws up her hands. "I saw the Grim Reaper, OK? I sound crazy. Maybe I am. But I *swear* to you when I lost consciousness and every time since, he's been there, talking to me."

"What does he tell you?"

"It's more like what he asks me to do. I have to learn lessons and pass tests. I meet people and they tell me things. They give me gifts, like realisations. Then I wake up and each time I do, I'm a little more human; a little more healed."

Curly gestures at her legs. "Physically?"

"No."

Curly turns off the device and sticks it in his top pocket. "I think we're about done here." He turns to his partner, eyes wide, mouth pressed in a firm line. "Let's go."

"You don't believe me."

"We never said we didn't, but it's our job to learn the facts and find the cause of the accident," Curly tells her.

His partner nods.

"It wasn't an accident. It was a murder slash attempted suicide. Are you going to arrest me?"

"We appreciate your time." He sighs and the officers turn to leave together.

Maria calls after them. "Wait! So you're *not* my third visitor?"

Curly leads the way as they exit the room, closing the door behind them, ignoring her. Through the glass panel, Maria sees them discussing the interview with Doctor Motley who shakes his head a lot, nods in understanding, then checks his watch.

They part ways.

What the hell just happened; am I not in trouble?

Either way, Maria is sure it will be the last she sees of those officers.

They weren't her last test.

But it won't be the last she hears of her sentence.

Chapter Twenty-One
WHEN YOU'RE ANGRY

Noah returns about an hour after the officers leave and when he enters, the circumstances are still confusing Maria. Why would they write her off like that, like she's crazy?

She isn't crazy, she's sure.

Crazy people need straight jackets and make strange noises, are violent and hear voices (at least they do on the television).

Maria is seeing and hearing Noah, so perhaps she *is* losing her mind. Then again, he sent her flowers with a little note card—flowers all the nurses and the doctor have seen and handled themselves.

He must *be real.*

He's real.

This time, Noah knocks on the door and Maria gestures for him to enter, though it's lazily with no excitement. Noah is astonished;

usually, she's thrilled to chat with him. She gets to argue about her feelings and intentions, yell and be unconscious for a while.

"Merry Christmas. I brought you some eggnog," he says, placing a pitcher of water at her bedside with a plastic cup.

"Turn my water to wine?" she grumbles.

"Ha-ha... drink up, doctor's orders."

"You spoke to my doctor?"

"I see all, hear all. I *am* all!"

"Yeah, yeah," she whines, sipping from her cup and tasting nothing but the plastic. She pulls a face. "Do you know when they will release me?"

"You're hopeful! You've only been in here a day, Maria. Didn't they tell you the 27th at the earliest? You've been in a serious car accident and frankly, you haven't exactly processed your grief fully."

"It wasn't an accident!"

Noah shrugs. "Arguable."

"Whatever."

"You don't seem as sad," he says.

"Of course I'm sad!"

Noah scrunches his nose. "Yeah, you look it. Aren't you the slightest bit angry at Marshal for what he did to you?"

Maria scowls and frantically shakes her head, then puts down her glass as if to prepare for confrontation.

Noah is suggesting Marshal harmed her when it was the other way around.

Marshal should be angry at her.

She should be angry at herself.

"He did *nothing* wrong."

"He left you alone in this world," Noah says. "Soon your mother will die and you'll be here on your own because your father won't be around much longer, either. Doesn't that make you angry?" He leans forward. "Because if it does, it's OK. Nobody would blame you. I'm a little angry myself; you needed your brother."

"He didn't leave me through choice, he fought to stay."

"And that makes you feel what? You're a troublesome person to read."

"Nothing. I miss him! I'm angry with myself for being so foolish. Everything seemed so clear and perfect; we would awaken with past relatives and live happily, in harmony, forever."

Noah stifles a laugh. "You *really* assumed you would sit on fluffy white clouds and play the harp all day? That surprises me."

"Why? Can't I have a pleasant delusion if it makes death more bearable?"

"Most humans do, so make up whatever little story you please." He waves a dismissive hand.

"Be assured it does *not* end that way. Marshal has already been through his options, Maria, and I can tell you he's happy. Marshal lead a strong existence and he did some charity work, he cared for his family and he had love in his heart. The circumstances of his death were tragic, the date of his death was tragic, and he didn't deserve to go so painfully. Christopher considered that."

"Christopher was his reaper?"

"Hmm. It didn't take Marshal long to learn the lessons planned for him. He's smart, that one. Chose an angelic afterlife, you'll be pleased to hear."

"He wasn't always an angel."

"No?"

"No! He was awful to me as a child and bullied me. In school, he never spoke to me. He'd embarrass me in front of my friends and scare me. On Halloween, he said he'd come trick-or-treating and instead he abandoned me and ran off with a bunch of girls from school who were all dressed way too skimpily for their age, then with his friends to smoke cannabis behind a shed. He cut the arms and legs off my dolls. He set fire to my hair once, too! He was a shit—got away with everything, denied it all and blamed most stuff on me or the dog. For a while, I hated him."

"Hate is a powerful word," Noah says. "I'm sure you loved him."

"Oh no, I didn't. Not until he matured and changed social groups. Then it wasn't so cool to pick on your sister—older sister, which makes this even more pathetic."

"Wait, you still wanted to go trick-or-treating in your teens?" Noah raises his brow.

"Don't judge me for clinging to my childhood, Noah. Besides, everyone on our estate did; as a community we loved Halloween."

"And what did your parents do about the way he treated you?"

"Nothing because they gave me the most attention—how could they punish him for acting out? He frustrated the hell out of me. I didn't want to live at home anymore and I couldn't wait until I went to university."

"So how did you end up living together?"

Maria exhales, releasing some of her concealed anger through her clenched fists.

It's been a while since she's talked about Marshal as a teenager.

"When he grew up, he changed. He got a job, got all serious about making a decent living and meeting a marvellous girl. Took up singing and playing the guitar, and he was pretty good at it! He wanted to marry, wanted children. He even apologised for the way he treated me once and I brushed it off."

"In song?"

"No, thank God!"

"Did you accept his apology?"

"Sure," she replies, lightly. "He's my brother after all and brothers like to wind up their female siblings."

"Sounds like you're still holding some of that anger in, though. Sounds like he had a nasty attitude. I'm on your side," Noah says, opening both palms, "but the question is, Maria, are you being honest with yourself? Are you holding onto the negative side of Marshal to give you something to hate? He died. He left you behind. He got the ending *you* wanted. He took your future and walked that path on his own. He could have held on for you or taken you with him."

Maria cries. "He didn't mean to. Do you think, wherever he is, whatever he's doing, that he forgives me?"

"It was Christopher who dealt with your brother's demise. I'm aware of what went on, but only Marshal can answer." He taps his heart. "Do *you* forgive *him*?"

"I didn't mean for this to happen. I was so confused."

"You didn't answer the question," he says.

"Do you forgive him?"

Maria pauses, then smiles. "I'd give anything to tell him I do. Do you think we will ever meet again?"

"You will."

She pauses and closes her eyes. "Noah?"

"Hmm?"

"Is Marshal *really* an angel?"

Chapter Twenty-Two
CLEAR MIND

Deflated, Maria struggles to sit upright in her bed. Her bruises are rubbing against the thin blue pyjamas the hospital has provided and her hair is greasy and matted. She longs for a more *luxurious* shower with steaming water, sweet-smelling shampoo and a fluffy white towel to wrap up in.

There's a gentle knock at the door and in strolls a nurse carrying what looks like a small plastic basin of boiling water, a bar of soap, a sponge and a flannel. Maria scowls, wondering if that's their best attempt at a relaxing bath following such a traumatic day. She'd even prefer for someone to wheel her into a wet room and leave her to it, though given her state of mind, abandoning her in a locked room with the ability to drown herself may not be the wisest of moves.

"I'm here to clean you up a bit," says the nurse.

Maria smiles as honestly as she can, but she's not looking forward to this. At least the nurse is friendly looking; she's perhaps 5'6" with ebony skin and braided hair, warm hazel eyes and delicate fingers. She'll be gentle, Maria knows, because being kind and caring is all part of her job description.

She must blush because the nurse says, "Oh, don't worry, hon. I'll pull the curtain 'round for some privacy. Alright?"

She nods. "Do this a lot?"

"Every day," the nurse says, smiling. She shakes Maria's hand. "My name's Gabriella. You're Maria?" She nods again. "Great. Can we take off this gown and I'll wipe your back? I want to be sure we get rid of any dried blood from your accident."

"It wasn't an... never mind."

Attempting to retain some modesty, Maria removes the gown and holds it against her breasts, blushing as the nurse tilts her forward slightly to wash her back, shoulders and neck. She takes extra care around her hairline where there is bruising; some hair is missing, which Gabriella imagines wasn't painful at the time but must now be tender.

"I've got some shampoo here; nothing too flash or designer, but it smells good and it'll wash away the past. Can you do this yourself, honey, or would you like me to help you?"

Maria considers how she'll rinse the soapy remains away once she's applied it to her scalp. Her head is itchy and uncomfortable to touch and though she's never suffered from dandruff or lice, she can't imagine the various breeds of gremlin calling her roots home.

She asks the nurse to assist with the rinsing. She disappears momentarily to find a jug.

"Makeshift shower head," she says, and winks. "I'll let you apply the shampoo so I don't hurt you. Then, you tell me when you're ready to rinse and I'll do the pouring. Just be sure to tilt your head back so we don't wet your sheets, though we can always change them later. OK, hon?"

Maria nods and holds out her shaking fingers. Gabriella squeezes out a dollop of orange cream, though it doesn't smell of oranges. It's wonderful when she massages it in until she hits a bruise or a cut or a matted knot and yanks the skin beneath.

She lets out a few *ouche*s and *ooche*s and *goddamnit*s.

The nurse never flinches.

"I think I'm ready," she says, "but is there any way we can comb through some conditioner? Do you have that here? It's just, well, if we don't, I'll probably have to chop it all off sooner-or-later."

Gabriella giggles. "I'll be right back."

And she is. Within seconds.

Maria wonders if there's a maid's cart or something out in the corridor like they use in hotels to replace the complimentary items in the bathroom. She returns carrying some sachets of white goo, but it instantly works its magic on her locks as she gently smooths it from root to tip.

"Now the next bit is more intimate so I'll leave the basin and the soap here for you, hon. I'll wait behind this curtain. Leave that conditioner in for a bit, eh?"

When the nurse leaves, she pulls down the sheets to reveal her lower half. It's ghastly. Her legs are vibrant—various shades of pink, purple, blue and green beneath various bandages. Her veins are spidery, like a web leading from her groin right down to her toes.

And the stench is overpowering.

After several days without bathing, Maria cannot imagine the state of her. She's embarrassed.

"How are we doing?" Gabriella prompts.

"Not so well, but I'm working on it."

Then she realises where the problem lies.

"Uh, Gabriella? I forgot—when the car... well it was my first day on… uh, on my—"

"On your period?"

Maria gulps. "Do you have any clean underwear and some, oh *why* is this so hard?"

She flings the sheets across her legs and sobs. Gabriella peers around the curtain and offers a weak smile.

"Oh, it's OK, hon," she says, moving the basin to the bottom of the bed and taking Maria's hand. "It's nothing to be ashamed of, and I've dealt with worse. Now, you wait right here and I'll be right back with some provisions."

She winks and disappears, ensuring the curtain remains closed. When she returns, she has some thick paper knickers and sanitary towels tucked under her arm, a bottle of feminine wash and some talc powder.

"We'll have you fresh and feminine again in no time. Do you want to do this yourself, or shall I help you?"

Maria's heaves get deeper and louder, and she shakes her head.

"This is degrading! How can you stand to be around me—the smell alone..."

"I don't mind, it's why I'm here. We've all

got to deal with our period sometime."

"Yeah, even those of us who can't have children. I hate getting my period at the best of times; it's a spiteful reminder of my failure as a woman," Maria hisses, then quickly apologises to Gabriella for being rude and ungrateful. "It's not your... I mean, thank you... oh, never mind."

"No apology needed, hon. You'll feel tons better when we've sorted it and next time you need a bath, you can ask for Gabriella and I'll come right back to help you again. Familiar face and all that."

Maria smiles and nods, wiping her nose on the material she's holding against her chest.

"I'm sorry you have to do this."

"I'm not," says Gabriella. "And you shouldn't be, hon. Femininity is something we have to be proud of and if messes like this result from being confident and independent—with or without children—then I say bring it on."

She gestures she's going to begin. Unable to handle the sight and smell of her own body, Maria looks away.

"It'll be over soon. It's not as bad as you imagined."

"Why did you want to become a nurse?" Maria asks, changing the subject to distract them both from the job at hand. She considers this thoughtful, almost angelic woman a blessing. "You always wanted to help people?"

"Was a nurse or a nun. My mind got made up as soon as I heard them nuns can't have sex."

Maria laughs between each sniffle.

Yeah, can't blame her for that one.

"You're religious, then?"

"Christian. Entire family is. Church on Sundays. Some might not enjoy it, but I do because it's bringing me to the person who created me, who knows my purpose and directs me for the greater good."

"Which is?" Maria asks, genuinely interested.

"To do more for his cause as a nurse than as a nun. And if the sex thing is an issue, well, he can take it up with me at them pearly gates by all means!"

Chapter Twenty-Three
NOT IN TROUBLE

"What did you think of your nurse?"

Maria stretches her arms and yawns. A presence rouses her from a restless sleep. She blinks repeatedly, strains at the morning sun as it hits her face and temporarily blinds her—between rays she catches Noah's silhouette at the bottom of her bed, arms folded and pacing. Another day; she made it through her first 24 hours as a paraplegic.

"She was friendly," she states, not knowing how else to describe a woman she's met only once.

She supposes words like empathetic and joyous might suit, but none of those words would fit Maria's usual vocabulary.

Instead, she states, "She was my third visitor."

"Only your third? Maybe I won't hire her as

your full-time carer, then. Not if she works for this lot—you've only had three people in here since the accident?"

"I don't understand—"

Maria shields her eyes with the flat of her palm. Instead of Noah's form, she sees her boss, Jude. He's the last person she expected, partly because she always saw him as a controlling bastard who could never remember her name, and partly because she'd always sort of fancied him and, so far, been relatively unnoticed unless he wanted a refill of coffee. But Jude is, admittedly, her ideal mate in the looks department. He's tall, dark and handsome (if a little sleazy and greasy-looking) with a Mediterranean skin tone, accent and a rich-guy-and-he-knows-it attitude.

"Sorry, I thought you were someone else."

"How did you manage that?" Jude says and winks.

"A bit confused, I think." She sighs and avoids eye contact. "Why are you here, Boss?"

"When I heard you'd been in an accident I had a quick whip round the girls in the office."

"I'll bet you did," she mumbles, thankfully inaudibly.

"So, what do you say?"

"It's kind of them to think of me."

"I'm not talking about the collection."

He throws a red envelope filled with change on Maria's bed, which lands on her leg. Unable to feel its weight, she growls and slumps back.

"There's a separate letter in there too, arrived at the office for you."

"Didn't you open it?"

"It's confidential," he replies.

"Oh, then thanks. Remind me again why you're here."

"About the nurse. Hiring her to be your carer."

Maria startles. "I'm sorry, I don't see why you're—"

"We want you back to work as soon as possible, Maria. I'm happy to pay for your care while you're under our employment if it means you can come back sooner and continue business as usual."

"That's a, um, *lovely* sentiment." She grunts. "Not sure if you've got the memo though, Boss, but I'll be going to prison and I'm paralysed. I'd take this as my notice."

Jude freezes and raises an eyebrow. "Since when?"

"Since I purposely crashed my car and killed my brother and put somebody's son in a coma!" Maria laughs. "Wow, you don't understand, do you?"

He's obviously not her third visitor, either.

Jude raises his hands. "Don't shoot the messenger, Maria, but you're *not* going to prison. I spoke to the doctor."

"But I'm guilty and—" Then Maria realises what he's just said. "Hang on. Why are *you* asking about my medical care; why is my doctor speaking to you? You're not family."

"You won't have much family left soon, so I'd be grateful if I were you." Jude clears his throat and instantly regrets lashing out. "I'm on your side—this job pays well and you're going to need the money. I merely asked if you were OK and the doctor said the Police had taken your statement and are releasing you once you're better. They thought I was your husband."

"That's a stupid mistake," she snipes.

"They're recommending you see a psychiatrist. I agree with them; something has troubled you for a while."

"Gee, thanks. Is there anything else you want, Boss? Forgive me, but I'm *not* in the mood for you to kick me right now. NOT THAT I'LL FEEL IT ANYWAY!"

Jude scowls and backs away from the bed. "I'm here to apologise that we didn't take action sooner and insist you take time away or something. Don't bite my head off."

"This isn't about work."

"We have a duty of care to our employees. If I overworked you—"

"Don't worry about that," she replies, turning away. "None of you need to take the blame or worry about lawsuits. Just get out. Consider this my notice—I don't need your charity or apology. You're not responsible for me."

Silently, Jude skulks out of Maria's room. He can't remember a time anyone spoke to him like that, especially by Maria who he's always held a soft spot for. She's pretty and hard-working, not like the other blonde-haired, skinny girls that constantly throw themselves at him every day.

Maria is classy and well-spoken, which is why he asks more of her than anyone else—she produces results, even if all he needs is a cup of coffee or something photocopying. She deserves her wage.

When he heard about her accident, Jude thought about how the company might run without her; he *did* ask a lot, and she completed menial jobs well below her pay grade. For the first few months he called her Mona, sometimes on purpose, because her capabilities threatened him.

When she'd attempted suicide, he panicked. Had stress at work or the way he treated her pushed her over the edge?

They *had* argued the other day...

Now, as he passes her doctor on the way out —a thin, blonde man who looks too young and gangly to be a qualified doctor—he heaves a disappointed sigh.

Maria groans aloud as the doctor enters. She reaches for the envelope and dumps it on the bedside table.

She's about to yell at him, too, for disclosing her personal information and medical records to her meddlesome boss, then swears when she sees the doctor is Noah.

He winks and clicks his fingers, rendering Maria unconscious for the last time.

Chapter Twenty-Four
SORRY, NOT SORRY

Maria is walking again when she opens her eyes. She's at the ward check-in desk beside two Policemen. It's Curly who speaks, explaining to the nurse at the counter how Maria will have to attend a psychiatrist for the foreseeable future and will remain under the care of Dr Motley.

But, she hears, there is no evidence to suggest she was, in fact, attempting to murder her brother. Whilst suicide is against the law, she's still here. There's no evidence to support the fault wasn't that of the guy in the coma for slamming into her, either—he should have maintained the correct stopping distance.

So, they've recommended a medical solution rather than a legal one.

"She had a rather nasty conk on the head," the nurse says, reading her notes, "and she's been talking to herself; I hear her on my rounds. Someone called Noah, I think. Arguing with him. When I check on her, she's asleep or in a bit of a daze."

"So, you agree?" Curly prompts. "She's unstable?"

Maria opens her mouth to argue, but Noah halts her by shaking his head.

They can't hear her.

They can't see her.

There's no point.

"I'm not sure she's completely with us," the nurse says in hushed tones. "We will assess her fully later. It's sad what happened to the other two, but she's blaming herself because she's guilty she's alive and they're... well... y'know."

"What, dead and in a coma?" Maria spits.

"You expected to be spending the rest of your life behind bars." Noah places a hand on her shoulder, but she shrugs him off. "This is excellent news. You're free to live your life without punishment."

"I don't want to live my life without punishment," she responds, "nor do I want to live my life at all! Not without the people I love."

"Plan kinda backfired, huh?"

Noah's eyes widen when she spins on her

heel, suddenly face-to-face with her tormentor. He takes a few steps back despite knowing neither can hurt the other, sensing she might need some time to think.

"And the lesson here is *what*, Noah? That you can *literally* get away with murder?"

There's an interminable pause.

Noah finally says in a whisper, "About that..."

"Oh, *what now*?"

"Well, you're not actually a murderer, Maria. I kind of lied."

Maria's breath catches in her throat.

Not a murderer?

"My brother is dead because of me."

"Your brother is dead because of a lamppost."

"I drove him into it."

"No, you didn't."

Maria folds her arms and closes her eyes, defeated. In the background, the voices of the Policemen and medical staff drift away, leaving her and Noah in a temporary, colourless space.

Noah tilts his head and half-smiles. "I need to show you something. You won't like it. You should. But, you won't."

Before Maria can ask further questions, Noah zaps them back to the scene of the crime, right before Maria hits the brakes, the car hits hers, and they all hit the post.

Maria is in the driver's seat, screaming at her brother to listen—she can ease his pain, she's promising.

What she actually said to him was, 'just let go and die already', which she's now regretting as Noah replays the scene from the back seat.

In the milliseconds left before the turning for the dock on the Hudson, something unusual flashes across Maria's face. Pain, maybe, though her expression is vacant like she's suddenly realising the purpose of mankind.

Her eyes glaze over.

She's sweating.

Noah rewinds the scene and plays it repeatedly until Maria's patience and sanity are on the edge.

"WHAT IS ALL THIS?" she finally cries.

"This," Noah says, "is the precise moment you realise you are not a murderer. You want to live. You want your brother to live. You've made a terrible decision and you're not sure how to back out. So, you do the only thing your human mind can do—you panic. You want it to stop. *Just stop.* And that's what you do."

"I stop," Maria whispers.

"You hit the brakes."

"Oh, my God. I don't even remember..."

Maria trails off, trying to comprehend how her subconscious made such a sudden life-changing decision for her. She can't remember making it or processing those thoughts, but seeing herself now in this out-of-body way, Noah is right.

"Are you OK?"

She nods.

"Are you sure?"

She nods again.

"Say something, Maria."

"What do you want me to say, exactly? You led me to believe I killed my brother."

"A 'thank you' might be nice."

Maria's eyes widen. "WHY WOULD I THANK YOU?"

"I have another gift for you."

PART THREE

The Choices

Chapter Twenty-Five
A VERY IMPORTANT JOB

✝

Still in the void, Noah conjures a small wooden table and two chairs which he invites Maria to sit at. He snaps his fingers again, retrieving a blue pen and a short, tea-stained contract from the nothingness. It's a single side of paper, no more, and there aren't many words.

"Now, about your afterlife..." he begins.

So *that's* what the document is for... it's her only option for being so nasty.

"What's the matter, don't you want to choose an afterlife? You've learned the lessons I wanted you to learn, haven't you? Been through the scenarios I wanted you to see? Don't you want your gift?"

"Was my boss visitor number three? It doesn't matter. There's only one thing on that bit of paper, Noah. You're not giving me a choice, you're giving me a sentence."

"A strange assumption to make when you haven't seen the contents. Then again, you humans are all about jumping to unnecessary conclusions."

"*You* were human once, Noah," Maria argues. "So those *aren't* my options?"

"They are." Noah grins. He's winding her up.

"You've spoken with Christopher already? But when; you've been here this whole time?"

Noah laughs. "*Really*, Maria?"

She shrugs and nudges her chair in a little, then crosses her hands on the desk, forgetting Noah is extended from Christopher, who is pretty much everyone and everything in the universe.

Simultaneously creating a table and chairs whilst discussing her afterlife with the all-knowing creator should be a doddle for him.

"It's easy for me to multi-task." Noah taps his head with the pen.

It shocks Maria—a sudden change of events and attitude on Noah's part. So, she gestures for him to continue; he'll lead her because there's nothing else she can physically do right now but sit and listen.

"Life has been unkind. Life has been unpleasant. Life has bullied you, Maria. Some suffer worse than others and some, like you, suffer the most. *I* was one of those people, too."

"When you fell off that building on 9/11," she prompts.

"The World Trade Centre's north tower. Christopher taught me the valuable lessons I needed to do the job I'm doing now. Sure, I had two other options, but he knew all along what I'd choose."

"Then why give you options?"

"Because they were mine to choose from. Free will is a very important thing."

Maria sits back. "Alright then, cards on the table."

Noah conjures two huge playing cards beneath his hands, which he spreads on the table. The first is a red Queen of the Universe rather than the Queen of Hearts, which he finds hilarious. The hearts become stars.

The second is the Joker.

She reaches out to flip them, but he halts her.

"There's no changing your mind. You played card games with your father, right?"

"When he was well enough."

"Good, so I don't have to tell you there's no point in bluffing."

The Queen of the Universe option is basic and as she expected. Noah wants to recruit her as Christopher recruited him all those years ago.

This time, there's an important twist.

He takes it in his hands and shifts the surrounding scenery, showing Maria the world's troubles in a 30-second presentation. She witnesses war, hunger and poverty, fear and anger. Cities. Towns. Villages. She sees people struggling physically, emotionally and mentally —some as she did. Hospitals and hospices, schools and universities, nursing homes, parks, playgrounds and religious establishments.

All at once, it fills Maria with the world's problems and her heart can't take the weight. She bursts into tears. Her troubles are petty and mediocre in comparison.

Noah shows how one thing causes many of the issues in Christopher's opinion (and therefore Noah's): religion.

There are too many people in the world believing in too many things. There are too many souls sucking the energy from the universe—from Christopher. They blame him for everything and he's finally decided he's had enough.

Noah wants Maria to be the solution as Christopher asked Noah to be all those years ago.

"After watching my little movie, it's

important you agree with its message if you choose this option. I need you to not only experience how the people of Earth are struggling, but how they are *causing* most of their problems. Christopher has known his actions so many years ago prompted the world's strife for a while. He introduced religion, giving humans something to believe in, uniting them. Instead, it drove them apart, creating more problems than they initially had. And, you guessed it, they *still* blame him, only in many forms."

"But religion is an outstanding thing. Why would you want to get rid of it?" Maria states.

Gabriella and her kindness were a perfect example; her faith brought joy and peace—helped her to care for others as a nurse.

Noah taps his pen, considering a way to explain in more depth, with clarity. "Belief in something greater than yourself is fine; Christopher is all around us all the time. Have I not proven that already? Religion itself isn't the problem, Maria, it's the war, the anger, the distrust and everything else caused by how humans have segregated and turned on one another *through* it. They use it as an excuse."

Maria reaches across the table. She squeezes Noah's hand.

"Like how you died?"

He pulls away. "Christopher once counselled a soul he wanted to fix it."

"Christopher's counselled *you*," she said, scowling, "and you turned down his offer."

"I did. At the time I wasn't sure if my decision would make a difference. Then I met you."

"Why would I want your sloppy seconds?"

"This is hardly sloppy! If you choose option one: *renewal*, Christopher Saint will absorb you the way I was—only, he will return you to Earth. You'll be re-born. Together, you'll become a solution to the problems he accidentally created the last time he meddled."

Maria grins. "The way you're meddling again now?"

"This is different," he insists.

"You're punishing me?"

"See it is a reward," he corrects.

"*You* didn't when he offered it to you. Plus, I'm not sure I want to return to Earth," Maria admits. "I'd rather see my family again—Marshal in particular. How will I... I mean, *Christopher*... fix the issues caused by religion, exactly? Will I remember this conversation? Will I remember my previous life?"

"He will make you a living reaper: a saviour. He wants to test if injecting some novel concepts slowly leads humans back to one another. For every soul you help, you will infect three others. And you will remember none of this. It's a fresh start, an alternative to being paralysed which I know you don't want."

"Infect them with what, Noah?"

His lips purse, then he says, "Infect the first with my concept: deference—each person they encounter will become infected and so on and so on."

"And the second?"

"Infected with Christopher's concept, on which I can say no more."

"Can I choose who I infect?" asks Maria.

"What would you want to do that for?"

"Y'know, some people are bastards."

Noah snorts through his laughter, making him seem, for a few seconds at least, completely human.

"Agreed. But no. It's like roulette."

"And the third?"

"The third what?"

Maria sighs. "The third person I'll infect!"

"They won't get anything. They'll live their lives as they do right now unless they come into contact with someone infected with either of the other two."

"That sounds risky."

Maria inhales deeply and leans back in her

chair. In the scenes she just witnessed, there were innocent children and hard-working families already suffering.

What if Christopher's concept is negative, or an illness—some kind of nasty disease or a virus that spreads?

What if it's death?

How can respectful submission to other people through deference fight something like that?

And those she doesn't infect with anything. Well, they're automatically screwed. Right? Humans are weak and selfish. Left to their own devices, they'll either get infected with Christopher's thing or nothing will change at all...ever!

"And you *really* can't tell me what Christopher's concept is? A hint or a clue?"

Noah shakes his head. "This road you must walk on blind faith alone. Both he and I are acting in the universe's best interest."

"I don't think I can do this. I've been a shitty human being so I get why he expects I'll be a good infectious saviour, but I'm not sure I can knowingly inflict something awful on people who've done me no harm."

"I never said Christopher's concept was awful."

Maria narrows her eyes and wrings her hands

together. He's starting to boil her blood.

"It's not free candy for all, though, is it?" She clears her throat and sits back. "Noah, let's get real—Christopher wants to kill off a bunch of troublesome people and will use me to get things moving, guilt-free."

"I'm sure he can just do that himself if he so pleases, but I guess we'll never know."

"Except you do, you just won't tell me!"

"Can't, not won't."

She throws her hands in the air. "What about my second card, the Joker, or is *that* going to cause religious genocide too?"

Chapter Twenty-Six
THE THIRD VISITOR

✠

Maria heaves and grasps for something to ground herself with as she's thrown back in the passenger seat of her little green car.

There are sirens in the distance and her windscreen wipers fight to clear thick falling snow.

She breathes steadily, watching grey mist swirl from her mouth for a few moments as she tries to figure out where Noah has dumped her this time.

When she looks down, Maria is wearing the same clothes and the clock on the dash says it's early afternoon, a few hours before she picks Marshal up for their day together. 'We Three Kings' is playing on the violin through her radio and without realising, she's humming along.

Noah Finn & the Art of Conception

The front door opens and Marshal steps out, locks it behind him and makes his way to her car. When he opens the door, the scene freezes and suddenly beside her in the passenger seat is a tall, broad man in a light grey suit and tie, which is brightly contrasting against the warmth of his coppery skin and hollow eyes. There's a handkerchief in his top pocket, blue like the one Noah gave her to blow her nose and wipe her eyes.

"Noah promised if you met your visitors and learned your lessons, he'd allow you to see Marshal again, pain-free. Am I right?"

Maria nods and swallows hard. "I've had my visitors: my teacher, the mother of the man in a coma and I think my nurse or maybe my boss, but it was less obvious. I told Noah I didn't need to see Marshal any more."

The man entwines his fingers in his lap. "He's an interesting soul, no?"

"Noah?" Maria half-smiles. "That's the understatement of the century."

When the man laughs, it's deep and throaty and his voice is older than his physical appearance seems.

"Did he tell you I once kicked him off a train? Not like law enforcement, but actually kicked with my feet?" She shakes her head, and he continues, "Well I did, and it was *hilarious*.

Deserved it, too. He ground my bones, that one. But it all worked out. I've been coaching him to take over the business."

Maria gasps. "Wait a second, are you...?"

"Christopher Saint," says the man, then offers her a handshake. "It's a pleasure, though perhaps not for you. Noah tells me you've fought him every step of the way; he's not sure you're ready to die, though he's confident you've learned something from your time here. He's rooting for you. Usually, reapers cannot feel—not as humans do. But with you? You're connected in a special way."

"Here in Limbo?"

"If that's what the kids are calling it these days."

"What else would you have me call it?" she asks.

Christopher winks. "Good girl, you're learning. Nice try."

"*You're* my third visitor, aren't you?"

He snaps his fingers. "You catch on quick. Your boss was a happy accident and the lovely nurse softened your pride a little. Noah just went with it. His initiative impressed me. Bonus points! Though, you didn't open your letter."

"The letter Jude gave me?"

"Hmm. A shame, because then this part would all make more sense."

"I don't care about any of that."

"You don't care why Noah worked so hard to save you?"

"I care more about why *you're* in my car right now and not him."

"It's the day of your accident," he tells her, though she already knows. "But it is also Christmas Eve. Familiar with the Christmas story, Maria?"

"About the birth of Christ?"

"Yes, good. In a few hours, you will say and do something silly. I've brought you here to kill two birds with one stone. Pardon the comparison," he quickly adds, "because I meant no disrespect."

"I'm listening."

Christopher jabs a thumb at the window, gesturing at Marshal who is, in super slow motion, getting into the car. If they don't hurry this conversation up, he'll be sitting on Christopher's knee soon.

"We're on the clock so I'll make this brief. You didn't kill your brother, Maria. You didn't kill yourself, either. Nor have you killed the delicate man in the coma."

"Emmanuel will live?"

Christopher nods. "That means you're off the hook."

"A hook I was never on because there is no

right or wrong, good or evil, Heaven or Hell, or even a 'hook'. Right?"

They laugh together but it takes Christopher a few seconds more to calm down; he has to reach for his handkerchief to wipe the sweat from his brow. She sees he's also shaking, and his presence flickers occasionally. There are some human traits mimicked for her benefit, she's sure, because why would Death need to sweat, be overweight or own possessions? Still, it causes her concern.

"Are you OK?" she asks.

"Fine, fine. I'm going to offer you something I've never offered another human soul before." He pauses for effect as he replaces the handkerchief neatly in his top pocket. "I'm giving you a second chance."

"I get to re-live the day?"

"Time is a funny thing—it moves and changes in unusual ways depending on who you are, and it's not linear. There are *so many* timelines in existence right now. You and Marshal, the versions of you you're aware of in here," he says as he taps her skull, "are on a single timeline and it's easy for me to bend— loop it around. We're running out of time. I can't explain any further."

"Running out of time?"

"Noah initiated your transition at 11:59 pm

on Christmas Eve. You're still there, Maria. Everything since has been carefully crafted to teach you necessary lessons. Should you choose the Joker card, Noah's timing will make more sense."

"The hospital wasn't real?"

"It's complicated," he says, smiling. "Noah agrees your circumstances deserved a one-off, limited edition kind of option. I've known for a long time what I have to do and put it off. It's rather drastic, you see. Whilst this option involves a bit of time-travel, the energy it uses would prompt the end of me."

"Surely, you can't die?"

"Nothing ever truly dies, Maria. But in this form, I can no longer exist. As you've noticed, my power is fading. I need your help to fix my mistakes. Noah already told you I created the concept of religion and injected it into humanity, but that action drained most of my energy. I've been recruiting helpers along the way; it's how Noah and I met. I offered to use the last of that energy to hire him as our planet's saviour but he declined. In the spirit of Christmas and as a favour to Noah, I'm offering the gift to you... in part."

"Ooh, a superhero?"

"Nothing so fantastical. A human being as before. If you will not allow me to test Plan A to deal with mankind by infecting them with what they are lacking, then I must attempt to reverse the damage through other means."

"You'll inject me with this infection and have me deliver it personally? Until now I never branded you as a monster!"

"Take it down a notch."

She flares her nostrils. "*Still* listening."

Marshal has moved about another inch since they started talking.

Time is running out.

"I can fix you, Maria," Christopher tells her.

He reaches over and places his palm flat against her stomach. His gaze meets hers and when he blinks, Maria feels a zap of electricity running through her body, collecting in her lower half, producing a warming sensation. It's pleasurable and soothing, exciting and like nothing she's ever experienced. She imagines it as a flame, burning brightly and hotter as the seconds pass until she can't bear his touch any longer and grabs his hand.

"I've decided to re-wind the clock to a time when mankind truly had a chance; you could have been wonderful! I want to embody all you have known and suffered, all you have learned and the people you've met on this journey into a fresh source of inspiration."

"What have you done to me? Did you fix my

legs? Am I bleeding?" she pants, panicking, and pats her legs and groin.

"If *you* will not help me resolve this, then I will recreate someone capable. Within you, Maria Shepherd, lies the solution to all our problems."

Chapter Twenty-Seven
JOKER

✝

Maria's eyes pool with tears. Something within her kicks and jolts her resolve; she grasps her stomach and, elated, cries out. She slams her fists against the steering wheel, causing the car to honk in slow motion.

It brings her back to reality.

She blinks and wipes her tears, surprised in these freezing temperatures they haven't instantly solidified.

"Is this a sick joke?"

Christopher shakes his head and smiles, pleased she's reacting positively.

"It is the Joker card, after all." He pauses to confirm, "No, I wouldn't do that to you. Maria Shepherd, you're pregnant."

"A *baby* is my second option? But how, when I'm on my—"

Noah cuts her off and shudders. "Women's troubles make me squirm, even in death."

"Try experiencing them!"

He laughs. "What... you think I can create a baby from thin air but I can't stop your period? *Please!* Give me some credit, Maria."

"But if I choose this, can you guarantee there won't be any complications—will my child be OK?"

"Perfect."

"Then I choose a baby!" Maria's face beams.

"Wait; this may seem like the better option on the surface but I urge you to consider both *in full* before you select. Either way, both solutions cannot instantly fix anything and we will probably lose further lives. People will struggle and suffer and the outcome we need may not even occur in his lifetime. But, in the long run, I pray this time Mankind can change."

"Oh, my God." Still stroking her stomach, she suddenly asks, "What would *you* infect the world with, out of interest?"

Christopher inhales sharply and his form flickers again. "All you have to do is honk once for Noah's offer or twice for mine to seal the deal. Those are your options. I *trust* you will choose well." He winks.

Marshal is almost in the car. It's time for Christopher to leave.

In a few minutes, she could either be re-entering the world as a newborn infectious baby —a saviour in the present tense—or live and give birth to a child who will do all that for her.

Maria bites her fingernails.

Can she knowingly put her child through such a responsibility?

"If I select the Joker card, will I remember my life here and our conversation?"

Christopher says, "Do you want to?"

"I think it could help. Then, I can teach my child what my visitors taught me; I can't forget or miss anything out. There's no excuse for our failure this time."

"I may have to switch the dynamics of my original plan a little," he sighs, "but your wish is my command."

Maria jumps and growls as Noah's irritating form replaces Christopher's glowing one.

If she never sees him again after her decision, it'll be too soon.

"Where did he...?"

"Did you miss me?"

"No," she grumbles. "I prefer your boss. He didn't mock or try to provoke me."

"That wasn't his job. Did he answer all your questions?"

"Not exactly. Can you guarantee...?"

"... no harm will come to your child because of his responsibilities? The answer is no. They will be able to suffer like anyone."

"How do you expect us to fix Christopher's mistakes, then?"

"When children are born, I give them traits and talents their parents can nurture or ignore. A kid wants to be an actor and their father tells them it's a waste of time. A kid wants to play the piano, so her grandmother pays for her to attend lessons. We are all born special, Maria, but life and the people we share it with can change our passions, even if those passions are things the world truly needs."

"You're giving my baby a passion for me to nurture, I understand. I won't let you down and I'll do my job."

"Christopher wants you to guide this child and nurture their unique talents. Or, as you say, passion. You should love them deeply, but remember that simply birthing them is *not* the afterlife we're offering or a ticket to tranquillity. Asking to remember everything that happened in this life kind of screwed up how well it will flow."

Marshal's body is now interfering with Noah's form. He's shuffling to allow room in the car, so decides the back seat is probably a wiser choice.

At the snap of his fingers, he's in the space behind, whispering.

"Remember the universe *always* delivers. It is a beacon, bright and guiding."

Maria sighs. "It didn't deliver for me. *You did*. Thank you for protecting me. Thank you for fighting for my future."

"This is not the closure you need, Maria," Noah's voice echoes as he fades. "It's a testament to how deeply you loved your family. But if I am to continue Christopher's work with a clear conscience, I need you to know why this meant so much to me."

Noah's form disappears, leaving behind an unopened red envelope marked 'confidential' on the dashboard.

Maria rips it open and stares at an unfolded birth certificate—*her* birth certificate—laid across her knees. A light blue sticky note hides some information but she sees her mother's name, Dylan, peeking from the edge.

And the note says: *I died so you could live.*

Chapter Twenty-Eight
60 SECONDS

✝

On Maria's dashboard appears a countdown clock.

There are only 60 seconds left of her journey through this nightmare.

In less than a minute, she must choose between reaping and infecting or living and parenting. The latter is what she's always wanted, but the former is what she deserves. Does she owe it to the memory of Noah Finn, the man who bravely died so she could be born to her biological parents, his ex-wife Dylan and her husband, Lewis?

Her options are in the best interests of the universe, *not* her well-being.

Her family history is the closure they both needed, she's sure. But, it's not what's important right now; no matter what she chooses, both paths are pre-approved by Christopher Saint.

That's all that matters.

"The way it should be," Maria utters.

Her heart is pounding.

She's sweating.

Thirty seconds.

What happens, she wonders, if she refuses to select an offer and allows time to run out? Will she cease to exist? POOF! Blown away like dust in the wind. Will he offer something worse for failing to appreciate Christopher's kindness and Noah's sacrifices, his willingness to bend the rules to save the daughter he never had?

Can she accept the Joker card if it will kill Christopher once and for all?

Flustered, Maria closes her eyes.

In her heart, there is only one option.

Maria honks the horn.

Chapter Twenty-Nine
WELCOME HOME

It's Christmas Day.

Maria is crying.

There's blood everywhere, thick and sticky and hot. Her forehead is slick with sweat and so are her palms, but people are grasping and squeezing them, offering her words of comfort and encouragement.

The pain! Oh, the pain is excruciating—already she regrets honking that damn horn. Already she's convinced she made the wrong decision.

"Ma—" she hears between the wailing.

The voice is soothing, and it's close-by, but faint, like she hasn't fully woken to her new afterlife or *previous life*, or worse.

"Ma—"

Beneath her is a crunching, rustling surface.

It's golden brown, softer than she initially thought, too. She knows the pain in her lower back is not because of the ground but because of the tiny human she's birthing. Each contraction sends another wave of panic and adrenaline through her veins.

There's excitement present within the myriad of emotions. It's what she's trying to focus on.

Wherever she is, it smells terrible and her nose is itchy. Despite the chaos surrounding her, Maria inhales sharply and inwardly curses Christopher for allowing her allergies to return like a twisted joke or Noah's idea of revenge. Her hatred of them both sufficiently distracts her until she hears a familiar, but unexpected, sound.

It's almost... *wait, is that a sheep?*

"Mar—" the voice calls out, louder this time. It tells her to push. To push harder.

Without knowing his name, she can tell the voice means the world to her. He's important. Family. She wants him here, and as he calls to her again, her heart latches on and cradles his presence like a comfort blanket.

She blinks through the sweat and gazes up past a circle of concerned faces into the sky, which is dark and star-filled, surrounded by a wooden border. There is no *way* she's giving birth in the garden or somebody's dirty shed!

Get me to a hospital!

She flings her arms out to brace herself and hoists her upper body into a sitting position long enough to see the baby's almost here. The head is crowning. A walk to a hospital or calling for an ambulance now would be impossible, so she slumps and spreads her fingers in front of her face to re-focus her vision. Though her sight is still foggy, she sees hay glued by blood to her palms in clumps.

Her nose twitches again.

"Ma—you're doing fine." The voice repeats, desperate for her attention. "Mar—keep pushing."

Maria's tiny frame can't take any more; it forces the baby out and into the arms of a man dressed in red and draped with a golden cloak. He unbuttons it from around his neck and wraps a crying boy tightly in it, folding the parcel like a burrito.

Maria screams one last time.

In a flash of silver, she regains her eyesight. The man in the cloak is almost three times her size, dressed in fine clothes and jewellery. His skin is the colour of rich chocolate dotted with amber freckles, but what draws Maria to him are those familiar eyes—mud brown and *hollow.*

He winks and hands the baby to a woman in a cerulean dress, then lays a mysterious bottle in the hay. Maria's attention snaps to the strange woman now holding her baby—a strong yet elegant blonde with poise and pretty ocean-coloured eyes. She's cooing at Maria's son, cradled in one arm as she hands another bottle to the woman beside her with the other.

The third stranger is equally beautiful but older in years. Her emerald cloak matches the glint in her eye, framed by curly and greying brunette hair. She kneels to discard the items; three thoughtful presents now mark the foot of Maria's makeshift bed.

Elizabeth, the rich woman in blue, brings a bottle filled with oil. She's travelled through time to purchase it and miles further to gift it. Its name reminds her of a child she lost in a terrible accident; she is determined to honour his suffering in this newer, simpler life—the baby boy she hopes, despite her age, to bare again.

From Francesca, the wealthy woman in green, is an aromatic earthy perfume to fill their lives with the wisdom she once endowed to hundreds of other children.

And from Christian, the man with the hollow eyes, is a decorative chest filled with gold coins

—a symbol of hope that this little boy will one day grow to be rich with knowledge, empathy and inspiration.

He will become a bold leader.

Finally, a man hands Maria the crying bundle. Her eyes fill with tears, focused so intently on the one thing she has always wanted.

She doesn't survey her surroundings. If she did, she might sooner realise shepherds and animals are witnessing the event. Sheep, mostly, but also horses, a cow and somewhere in the back, a scurrying chicken.

Her husband, the man who called her name before, pats her shoulder. He's a patient, bearded carpenter wearing a single grey garment.

"Joey?" she whispers. Her breath catches in her throat. "*Joseph?*"

Joseph cries, "Mary, darling, he's perfect!"

Chapter Thirty
THE SAVIOUR

✝

Mary lays back in Joseph's lap, staring through a hole in the thatched roof directly above them. The night is calm and clear, scattered with tiny twinkles, some of which gather to form a diamond-shaped beacon that illuminates the saviour in a single spotlight.

Their first light.

It is bright, and it is guiding.

She nestles her newborn son against her chest for the first time.

She promises to love him with all that she is —all she will ever be.

And in the distance, an angel sings.

DEDICATION &
ACKNOWLEDGMENTS

Maria Shephard's death was another difficult story to write because it explores bitterness, regret and abandonment. Life's challenges and our personal differences can sometimes force us apart; we detach from what's truly important, find reasons to hate and blame one another for what we are unable to control—acts of God.

Though I'm not particularly religious, I find writing about the meaning of life and death fascinating, and do believe we have a purpose, even if none of us are sure what that purpose is.

I want you to know the universe values you, no matter your circumstances or troubles, your past, or what's yet to come.

There is a Christopher for every Noah, and a Noah for every Maria. I'm grateful every day for mine.

To my Christopher Saints and Noah Finns: I love and appreciate all of you.

♥ Thank you for everything.

Additional thanks must also go to:

★ my editors, proofreaders and BETA readers as always. Thank you for all your hard work!

★ & my loyal readers. Thank you for buying this book. I hope you found comfort and meaning in its pages.

ABOUT THE AUTHOR

E. Rachael Hardcastle is an Amazon #1 bestselling author from Bradford, UK.

Despite running a publishing house for new writers, Curious Cat Books, from West Yorkshire in the UK, Rachael is still a writer at heart, sharing important morals and values with the world through her fiction. And she loves sharing her passion for writing through school and community visits!

Out of the office, Rachael is an avid reader of various genres, a lover of cats, coffee, stationery and her trusty bullet journal.

www.erachaelhardcastle.com
www.curiouscatbooks.co.uk

**If you enjoyed this title,
please consider leaving a review
on your favourite retailer's platform.**